ALSO BY PAMELA RAFAEL BERKMAN

Her Infinite Variety

The
Falling Nun

AND OTHER STORIES

Pamela Rafael Berkman

Illustrations by Karen Roze

A TOUCHSTONE BOOK
PUBLISHED BY SIMON & SCHUSTER
New York   London   Toronto   Sydney   Singapore

TOUCHSTONE
Rockefeller Center
1230 Avenue of the Americas
New York, NY 10020

"The Falling Nun" first appeared in the 1998 issue of *Faultline*.

TOUCHSTONE and colophon are registered trademarks of Simon & Schuster, Inc.

For information regarding special discounts for bulk purchases, please contact Simon & Schuster Special Sales at 1-800-456-6798 or business@simonandschuster.com

Designed by Kyoko Watanabe

Manufactured in the United States of America

1 3 5 7 9 10 8 6 4 2

Library of Congress Cataloging-in-Publication Data
Berkman, Pamela.
The falling nun and other stories / Pamela Rafael Berkman ; illustrations by Karen Roze.
p. cm.
Contents: Tat—Gold glitter—Veronica—Snakes—The falling nun—Bethlehem—Witch—Men have more upper body strength—Holy holy holy—February 14—Playing crucifixion—Merry Christmas, Charlie Brown.
1. Young women—Fiction. I. Title.

PS3602.E757 F3 2003
813'.54—dc21   2002029210

ISBN 0-7432-3019-1

To my family

CONTENTS

Tat

W h e n Liberty walks into Ed Hardy's Tattoo City, she is
already not as she was when she came into this world. She drips
with jewels the way a tropical bird drips with colored feathers.
She is dotted all over with little golden rings. It is as if she is covered inside with a fine spiderweb of lacy wires, and the precious
gems and bright metal where the web is anchored peek out here
and there to decorate her. There is a diamond nose ring, a delicate circlet through her belly button, amethyst and garnet studs
in the tender tabs of flesh inside her ears. Her body is embroidered. She is crewelwork, filigree.

But it is not enough. The piercings are beautiful, but they are
over too soon. They are too easy, too common; they don't leave
enough of a mark. They don't do what she needs them to do.
They don't say what she needs them to say. She is not entirely
sure even what that is.

Bzzt, bzzt, bzzt, she hears. *Bzzt, bzzt, bzzt.* One of the two tattoo artists is finishing up a job. In an open cubicle, a very young
man lies on a padded table with his pant leg rolled up. He is covered knee to ankle with a great, gaping trompe l'oeil wound.
Crushed bones, tattered muscle, tendons, sinews, blood, and
machinery show up on his flesh as though he has been skinned.
The artist is rubbing more pinkish color onto a strip of muscle
with a tattoo gun that looks like a tiny pistol. The young man is
not squirming. Liberty wonders if it will hurt so little when her

turn comes. Maybe by now he is used to it. He must have been on the table for hours receiving that monstrous tattoo, the outline first, then the color added, creeping into the picture like a flame along the edge of a newspaper.

"Just a minute," says the guy at the desk, who Liberty now realizes is not a second artist but only the helper. Under his T-shirt his arms are solidly red, blue, and green, the decoration stopping abruptly at his wrists, tattoo sleeves.

"That must hurt," Liberty says, jerking her head toward the guy on the table.

"He was in an accident last year. He's got all this metal in his leg."

"Yeah?"

"It's like he wants the outside to show the way his leg is on the inside. To honor it."

"Cool."

"So what can I do for you?"

Liberty unfolds the elaborate antique valentine. The helper calls over the tattooist. The guy with the metal in his leg just lies there.

"I wanted it a little smaller," Liberty says.

The artist shrugs. His name is Igor and he is from Denmark. It says so on a little flyer on the wall with the other brochures and qualifications of all the artists who work at Ed Hardy's Tattoo City.

Igor is holding up his rubber-gloved hands like a surgeon. He wears a Greenpeace T-shirt and his arms are covered with pictures of beautiful dark-haired women in swirling ocean waves. Would I see myself in there, Liberty wonders, gazing at his skin, wondering if a face like her own is there among the tides and eddies, if the inky water circles around hips like hers there on his biceps, and is then surprised that she has had the thought.

"You would lose a lot of detail," he says. He speaks formally, almost without contractions, in his Danish accent. "Honestly, I would not cut it down much. I like it very much. It is from where?"

"Just a street fair." Liberty is flustered with the flattery of the tattoo artist approving her choice. "Around last Valentine's Day, down by Saint Columbus's. This guy had a whole card table of them."

Igor tells her, "I love old prints and papers."

"Do people bring in a lot of them, to get copied?"

"People bring in everything."

Still holding his hands up, Igor watches while the helper at the front desk turns over the time-softened card. It is faintly perfumed, even now.

"Where?" Igor asks.

"I was thinking right here." She runs her fingers over the papery skin between wrist and elbow on the inside of her right forearm. "Will it hurt there?"

"It will sting anywhere you get it." He studies the lines, the cherubs, the roses, the curlicues. There is a romantic verse beneath the illustration. "You want that, also?" he asks, pointing, and she nods. "Wearing your heart on your sleeve, huh?" He grins.

"I guess."

He heads back to the padded table. "I can begin in one half hour," he calls over his shoulder, not to Liberty but to the guy at the desk. *Bzzt, bzzt, bzzt.*

"You can sit down," the guy says.

"I really might want it a little smaller," she says again. She has envisioned a floral, feminine accent to her golden skin and glistening jewels, not a big, full-blown butchy tattoo.

"No, you don't want to do that." It's the guy lying on the table speaking, and Liberty notices that his teeth are clenched and his voice is strained. He hurts after all. "Little tattoos just look stupid. You're going through all this, you know, *pain*, and you don't want to end up with just a colored freckle."

"Well, I didn't mean like a freckle," Liberty calls over to him.

He goes on talking. "It's important. They spread. They're always gonna spread. They get fuzzy. Get it as big as you can.

They spread inside of you, too. They become more and more part of you."

Igor continues with his work, oblivious. *Bzzt.*

"First one?" the tattooee says.

"Oh, yeah." Now that he is talking to her, she feels it is okay to look at him more undisguisedly. His arms and shoulders are covered, not like the guy's at the desk, not like sleeves, but with the classic pictures, the topless hula dancers and the hearts with banners. The face of an old-fashioned nurse with a red cross on her cap peaks out from a blooming rose. The blue and green shades on the Polynesian scenes are already dim and faded. He is so young, Liberty thinks, even a little younger than she is; these tattoos are almost from childhood. Illegal.

She can think of nothing else to say to him, so she asks Igor, "Should I go and get a drink? Tequila or something?"

"It won't help. It will only make you bleed more."

It will only make her bleed more. She sighs.

The guy at the desk says, apparently by way of soothing her, "He's the best. He's teaching me."

She turns to look at him. "Really?"

"Yeah. I'm his apprentice. I've already done twelve tattoos."

"On who?"

"My first was on my brother."

"What was it?"

"A winged serpent. Red and orange. Fiery."

She's tensing up. For her piercings they could always see her right away. She keeps talking.

"Do you like it?"

"Oh, yeah. It's so much better than the bank. I work at Bank of America. Days. 'Cause they don't pay me to work here, it's in exchange for my training."

"What do you do? At the bank?"

"Dunning calls." He makes a face. "I fucking hate it."

"But you like the tattooing?"

"Oh, yeah."

"Really? What makes you like it so much?"

He pauses but then decides to answer her. "Everyone's so grateful, you know? They look in the mirror when they're done, and you can tell they're thinking, 'Right on, man, I did it.' They just keep telling you thanks and saying how beautiful it is."

He's flushed, his eyes open wide. "Well, you know," he finishes. He looks away to fumble with some useless paperwork on the desk and Liberty notices how close shorn his dark hair is, how soft it looks.

"What made you want one?" asks the young man from the table.

Liberty turns her head to look at him. She had forgotten about him.

"I don't know," she says, and she doesn't. She knows that part of why she likes the piercings is that they belie that her skin is undamaged and whole, that she herself is unpunctured. She knows that everyone is punctured. She thinks the piercings are sexy, and she hopes the tattoo will be, too.

Liberty is quite beautiful. She is tall and dark and warm looking, with heavy brows and heavy hair. All her baubles look right on her, they fit her, as though she is a princess from some ancient nation.

Bzzt, bzzt.

She has a sudden sense that she should check into the safety of this operation, and walks over to the apprentice's desk.

"Can you tell me something? Do you guys use disposable needles?"

"We make all our needles by hand," he says. "Because machine-made needles can have barbs, you know?" He demonstrates barbs, holding two fingers up together and bending one. "And you don't get a clean line." He is obviously proud to say this. "We have to throw them away after. There's a law."

"What's in the ink?"

"Hey, Igor! The lady wants to know what's in the ink."

"I do not know. Something organic." Igor nods to the kid on his table, who doesn't see him because his eyes are tightly closed.

Then he takes off his rubber gloves and washes his hands in a little stainless-steel sink next to him. He puts on new rubber gloves
and gets a box of Saran Wrap from a drawer. He pulls out a big
piece of it and wraps it in several layers around the decorated leg,
anchoring it with white cloth tape. The guy sits up, opening his
eyes. They're blue.

"Jack, do you want the instructions?" asks Igor, holding out a
yellow Xeroxed sheet. Jack's the guy with the metal in his leg. And
those, Liberty thinks, are the directions on how to take care of a
new tattoo, like the kind they hand out at piercing parlors, with
the part pierced checked off. "Earlobe . . . cartilage . . . eyebrow . . .
navel . . . labia . . . clitoral hood . . . Prince Albert . . . triangle . . .
apadravya . . ." She had once asked what the incomprehensible
ones were, but the woman on duty at the time had been snippy
and would only say that they were for men.

Jack does not want the instructions. Liberty watches him
once his pant leg is rolled down to see if he is limping. He is not.
He sees her watching him and says, "It stops hurting as soon as
they finish. It itches for a while, though."

Igor is still cleaning up. "So not small?" Liberty says to Jack.

Jack shakes his head vigorously. Jack, Liberty realizes, is a little goofy, or at least in a goofy mood. "No," he says.

The apprentice is smiling wickedly at her. He is relishing this
moment. Liberty thinks he must relish it every time.

"You're up," he says.

She shakes herself all over, as though she is just waking up,
and heads over to the table. She is wearing overalls over a cardi-
gan sweater and she takes down the bib so she doesn't have to lie
on the buckles and pushes her sleeve up over her elbow.

"No friend coming?" asks Igor. "Some people like a friend."

"I want to surprise them." And there is no one she really feels
close enough to, not to bring along for this. She's between
boyfriends, and her girlfriends, while helpful in times of breakups
and reassuring during discussions about food, anorexia, and female
body image, are all careful not to appear too needy to each other,

not to break an indefinable but nevertheless collectively understood barrier. Liberty is the most pierced of all of them. They
would not think she would need them for this.

She feels flirtatious, probably from nervousness. It was not
good to sit and think about it, to hear the needle and anticipate.

"He didn't need a friend," she says, nodding at Jack.

"It wasn't my first one," he says. "Igor, can I use your bathroom, man?"

When he comes back Igor is still tracing the complex valentine onto special paper which he runs through a machine with a
roller that turns it into a soft purple outline.

"I'd like kind of muted colors," says Liberty. "To match the old
paper, you know, not just tattoo red and tattoo green."

Igor nods and Liberty is unsure whether he understands or is
simply dismissing her. She would not mind an advocate of some
kind.

"I'll hang out," says Jack. "You want me to?" His backpack is
already slung over one shoulder but he swings it off and puts it
on the floor.

"You're gonna make sure he doesn't write 'Mom' on me?"

"Or something." So Jack straddles a chair in the tiny cubicle.
Igor has dipped the paper with the soft purple outline in water
and he presses it to the inside of Liberty's arm, then carefully pulls
it off. It leaves its print, like in a color-by-number kit, on her flesh.

"Okay?" he asks.

Liberty looks, but not too closely. The decision is made and
she can't bear to start fussing with niceties.

"Okay," she says.

Igor begins. With the first short burst of cutting pain he has
drawn a short black line and now she has to stay until the end.

It is like a knife. Liberty is surprised at how simple the feeling
is. It is like a knife, nothing else, a small sharp knife cutting into
her flesh the outline of the heart, the cherubs, the flowers and
curlicues, the brief verse, all in black. *Bzzt, bzzt, bzzt,* she hears
again. Only now it's her.

She can't watch—she never watches her own piercings, either—but she knows it doesn't look like a paring knife, this instrument that is deliberately, and not particularly quickly, drawing in her own blood on her forearm. She had expected a prick, a needle sharpness. She had known there would be something, but she didn't know how high the level would be. She thinks this must be what the beginning of a stabbing feels like. She doesn't want to open her arm to Igor. Her body strains away, but she forces the forearm to lie still and the tension between these two things stiffens her neck and shoulders.

She remembers that during piercings she is always instructed to take a deep breath and then let it out slowly and completely when the needle goes in. She tries this, but her breathing gets faster and faster and finally Igor says, "Do not hyperventilate on me now. It is not good for you to pass out."

"Sorry," she says, and laughs nervously, tightly, with pain, at the very low end of hysterical. Every second that the needle is off her is a respite. What Jack said is true; it only hurts when the needle is on you in this stop-and-start operation. As soon as the fine silver point is withdrawn, the pain stops. *Bzzt, bzzt, bzzt.*

During a pause, Liberty looks at what has happened to her skin. The valentine is about halfway outlined in black. One of the little cupids is missing his face, and the curlicue lines still need to be done, along with the second half of the double heart, and some flowers. But one whole heart, most of the roses, a couple of cherubs, and the verse are finished.

Hail, Bishop Valentine, whose day this is;
All the air is thy diocese.

This is what it says on Liberty's skin.

"Has anyone ever just said they can't take it and gotten up and left?" she asks.

"Sometimes," says Igor. "But not very often."

"Yeah . . . I guess you're kind of stuck."

Igor resumes the cupid's face.

"You can say 'ow' if you want," says Jack.

"Ow, ow, ow," Liberty obliges, her legs and free arm squirming. "I guess I don't have to say ow. I could say something else. Zen, Zen, Zen . . ."

Jack, she notices, is now taking deep, slow breaths with his eyes closed.

"What are you doing?" she says, irritated. Everything is irritating. *Bzzt, bzzt, bzzt.*

"Tonglen," he answers. "It's this really cool form of Buddhist meditation."

"What is it?" asks Igor.

"The idea is that you take on other people's pain and you send out good energy to them," he says. "You imagine all their pain and anger and humiliation or whatever, and you imagine yourself breathing it in. And then with the out breath you imagine that you're sending them good, calming energy."

"What if you don't like the person?" asks Liberty.

"You have to start with someone you like. People you don't like are harder. Usually you start with yourself, and then you expand on it."

"So what is the point?" says Igor, smiling. "Does it make the person feel any better?"

"I don't know, man, okay?" says Jack. "Jeez. It's about compassion."

"I guess the idea is kind of to increase the sum total of kindness in the universe?" says Liberty. "Right?"

"Something like that."

"Are you taking on my pain?" she asks, squirming.

"Of course."

"Thanks. But I still feel it. Zen! Zen! Zen!"

"That looks great. Are there any you can't do, man?" asks the apprentice, who is watching admiringly from a little distance away. Liberty has forgotten about him, but since no one else has come in after her, he is free to watch.

"Anything racist," says Igor, which is not exactly what his apprentice meant. "I will not do anything racist."

"That hadn't even occurred to me," says Liberty. Her body has calmed down a little. The pain is now just below her threshold of what is bearable, instead of just above it, like it was before. Her neck and shoulders are still aching and she hates leaving her vulnerable wrist on the table to be poked at more, but she might have gotten a little used to the feeling after all.

"Oh, yes. There are many packs of young Aryans who come in wanting swastikas. They like to put things like 'Die Nigger' onto their skulls." Igor withdraws the needle. "Time for the colors."

Liberty sits up. Her overalls fall down to her hips and she sees the apprentice starting with surprise, staring for a second at her torso, her silky belly, and then blushing. But he collects himself.

"How you doing?" he asks.

"Do you think," she answers, "I could have a glass of water?"

Igor is busy mixing inks in Styrofoam cups. He mutters, "Can you, Shermie?" to the apprentice. So that's his name. He fills one of them at the sink and gives it to Liberty.

"I'm sorry it's Styrofoam," Igor says.

"Oh . . . I don't care."

"I do."

"Oh. Sorry."

Liberty takes deep, slow breaths.

"Nice," says Jack, pointing to the gold ring studded with a white sapphire through her navel. "What do you think, Igor? You like that?"

Igor shrugs. "Yeah, it's nice."

"You don't like it? You're not into the piercing thing?" Liberty asks. She is particularly proud of the belly button ring. It was her first body piercing. She was told that gold navel rings were signs of royalty in ancient Egypt.

"When you come down to it," says Igor, "it is just a ring. This is art."

Jack wiggles his eyebrows at Liberty. "Igor," he says, "is a purist."

"This will feel different than the outline work," Igor is saying. "This will be more of a numbing sensation."

He takes the cup from Liberty and she lies back down. "Tell me if this is the kind of color you want," he says. Liberty can feel the night, the dark blue of it, not unlike Jack's eyes above her, creeping in, cool, around the edges of the door and through chinks and cracks in the tattoo parlor drywall.

She gasps when Igor touches her with the wider, rougher bit that he has put into the machine. Its surface is a tiny oval paved with needles. It feels like the gravel forced into her skin when she was eight or ten and fell off her bike in the driveway, only deeper, and it doesn't help at all that the gravel now seems to be made of dark rubies and emeralds. The dust of precious gems is particularly hard and sharp ground into the flesh.

"Not numbing, huh?" Jack says.

"Is this the muted you mean?" asks Igor. Liberty turns her head to look. The strip of color in the heart is a brighter, more vermilion red than she had wanted.

She gulps. "Well, actually, I was thinking of something a little . . . smokier."

Igor mixes some other inks in another cup and tries again on a new strip of skin. Liberty tries to will herself to become used to this feeling, too.

She looks. The color is a deep, muddy garnet. "Oh, yeah. That's perfect!" she says with real pleasure. He begins, and the heart is filled without further event, as are the purple and lavender wings of some insectlike fairies. But Liberty cannot keep her breath when Igor begins on the olive-green flowering vines. She clicks her shoes together and begs Igor, "Why does it hurt so much again?"

"It's a new area," he says.

"It might be because the vines are so narrow, and the skin's already irritated near the outline," Jack offers. "And you could have a nerve line there. Everybody's different."

"You guys don't have any anesthetic or anything at all, ever?"

"Oh, no," Igor says. He shakes his head. "You should experience it. After all, how many times are you going to do this?"

"Once," Liberty snaps.

Igor and Jack and Shermie the apprentice all laugh. "That's what they all say," says Jack. "You'll be back."

"Zen!" cries Liberty. "Zen, Zen, Zen! Jesus fucking Christ! Zen!"

Shermie steps up close to her head. "Tell her about the weirdest tattoo you ever did."

"Yeah," says Jack. "Tell her about the weirdest tattoo you ever did."

Igor grins slightly, working away on the rose-laden vines. "This guy came in," he says, "and he wanted the stigmata."

"Wow," says Liberty, really quite impressed with the weirdness.

"Wanted it all tattooed right on him, right, Igor?" says the apprentice. "Hands and feet and everything. He wanted some drops of blood on his head from the crown of thorns."

"Did you do it?" asks Liberty.

"Oh, yes. Everything except the lashes on his back," Igor answers. "I did not have time for them that night and then he said he would come back but he did not. I charged him six hundred dollars. The wound in the side was very challenging, to make it look real."

"Jesus God. Why did he want that?"

"I do not know."

"I wonder if he was trying to pull some scam."

"I did not ask him."

"Maybe it wasn't a scam," Jack says. "Maybe he felt like he really wanted the wounds of Christ. It could happen. I believe stigmata could happen, sometimes."

"I do, too," says Liberty. Her voice is higher than usual. She doesn't want to talk. She is concentrating on containing the pain, keeping it somewhere in the very center of her brain and not letting it out. "But not if you get it tattooed on. That's kind of fraudulent. . . ."

"In medieval times they would have thought that was okay.

They thought the point was that you wanted to share the same, you know, physical pain as Jesus. It was cool if God gave it to you, but it was okay to do it yourself. You know how they used to flagellate themselves."

He stops, then bends over to unzip the backpack at his feet. He fishes among dozens of yellowed paperbacks, books like those Liberty sees for a quarter each at the Salvation Army store. One is the *Poetics of Aristotle*, she sees, one is *The Magician's Handbook*, with a top hat and deck of cards on the cover. He finds the one he wants, fans its pages beneath his fingers, hits one of many corners folded down. He quotes: "The love and suffering of these souls 'oned' with Jesus Crucified, so overflows that the very wounds and marks of their Crucified Lord appear in mortal bodies. Here we seem to find the clue to one of those marvels of God's power that has most strongly impressed the imagination of human kind; certainly no other supernatural manifestation of an external kind has proved so arresting as this; an altogether extraordinary love of the Crucified, joined to an equally extraordinary desire to be like Him, to feel what He felt, and endure in the body what He endured, as far as such is possible for a creature. Love explains all."

He stops again, puts the book in his back pocket as though he wants to keep it handy, and smiling with pride chirps, "Father Benedict Williamson. *Supernatural Mysticism*. Nineteen twenty-one. Love explains all."

"That is very nice, Jack," mutters Igor.

"Igor, I'm not sure I can handle this," Liberty hisses, very fast. He takes the needle away. "Well, what do you think? It is up to you. We can take a break or I can try to finish it up."

"No, I guess," says Liberty. "I guess just finish."

"You're getting there," says Jack.

"Almost there," says Shermie.

Igor makes the cheeks of the cherubs pink, the points of their arrows powder blue. *Bzzt.*

Igor stops. Igor is finished. The tattoo is finished. It is a second before Liberty knows it. "You're done?" she asks, and her whole body turns to mush, her very finger joints watery with relief from the tension she hadn't realized they were holding. She sits up— "Not too fast," says Igor—and looks at her lower arm in wonder, the way she would look at a Fabergé egg in a museum.

The colors are deep and soft and solid. The angels and fairies burst out from her skin, flying up and down and around. The flowers hang down heavily over the hearts and the lacy edges flutter over her wrist. The verse is large and clear in old-fashioned handwriting. She smiles up at Igor, laughing, almost bashful. She's glad it's big. Who would have wanted a tiny, delicate tattoo? That would have been no different from another gold ring.

She is unprepared for the feeling of accomplishment that surges through her. She did it. By God, she really did it.

Liberty suddenly realizes that she likes getting tattoos.

"Thank you. It's beautiful," she says. "It's perfect. Thank you."

"It'll never look quite like that again," says Shermie. "They never look as good as the day you get them."

The instructions on the yellow sheet say not to sit in chlorinated hot tubs or saunas until she heals. They say the area will itch, like a sunburn. They say wash it, don't scrub it, in a few hours and cover it with Neosporin. Liberty writes Igor a check for a hundred and twenty-five dollars.

"I have to say it's the prettiest one I've seen," Jack says, staring at it closely with his head tilted.

"I liked doing it," says Igor, shaking Liberty's hand. "Come by and let us know how it is doing." He turns to a drawer beneath the sink. "Let me take a picture," he says, smiling. "Maybe we will put it in my book." He produces a Polaroid camera from the drawer and snaps Liberty's wrist and inner arm, still seeping blood, before he wraps them in plastic. She gazes at the picture, standing and buckling her overall straps, while the lines of her new tattoo become clear.

"Remember," says Jack, "you go out that door a brand-new person." This close to him she can smell him, his own scent mingled with the antibacterial soap on his leg, and see that on his hands are inscribed the words "Hold fast," one letter on each finger.

"Why?" she says. She points to them. "Why 'Hold fast'?"

His face is startled. For some reason he had not expected such a question. "For sailors. To remind them to hold on, hold on really hard to the rigging, not fall overboard."

She looks up at him and his eyes are very blue. It seems as though he makes everything around him blue just by looking at it. Liberty understands now why Jack waited with her when his turn was over, why he tried to ease her pain. The cuts and burning have opened her up, and she has never felt so full of love and welcome for all human beings who step across her path, never felt so undefended and so unneedful of defense. She will tell anybody anything. She will listen to anything anybody has to say. She will help whoever asks her, she will give anything for which she is asked. In her mind, while she looks at his eyes, she kisses Jack, opens her mouth underneath his, and in those eyes she sees that he knows this, that he is there, too.

She walks out into the night, full of joy at the pink flowery wound across her wrist. The air is clear and liquid and she feels she is at the bottom of an overturned bowl of stars. Years later, waking up next to Shermie, an apprentice no more, when their lives have already ebbed and flowed together, shifted and reshifted and shifted again, she will remember the warmth that pulses through her this night, so that she glows golden in the cold dark blue. It seems to her that everyone she knows is so full of love and suffering, so very full, that it overflows into wounds, and at last she is not an outsider, and never will be again. She knows now what she wants all the intricate jewelry, all the wounds real and artificial on her body, to say. She wants to say, "I do love. None of us are whole, but I do love. Love explains all." She needs to fall in love now, to find someone to love with all her soul.

Gold Glitter

Elizabeth went dressed to kill Halloween night. There was a party at a bar, at this dive called The Touch. She always had a weakness for glitter, for shiny Christmas cards and sequins and gaud. Some child's love of sparkling tutus and fairy princess dresses. So all over her skin and hair, under her black pavé sequined strapless dress, under her black lace witch's hat and her black lace stockings knit like spiderwebs, under her fake pearl and ruby jewels and white kid elbow-length gloves, she wore Jerome Russell Hair and Body Glitter gel in gold, and she was luminous. A little boy in ninja gear saw her on the way to The Touch with her friends and cried out, "She's glittering! Ma, she's glittering!"

It smelled good and it was edible, the bottle of glitter said. Should it ever come up.

Joshua had dumped Elizabeth a couple of days earlier.

"It's just not working for me. I don't think it's going to. I don't know why. You're really great. I'll never forget you. Let's be friends."

Elizabeth never argued. Not with such overwhelming evidence against her. Just let it twist around in her throat. It never helped to talk it out. Never.

Vinnie wore horns to The Touch that night. They were delicate and tasteful, flesh-toned, like a faun's, just elegant little buds curved ever so slightly inward. Elizabeth realized later that they were more elegant and suave than he was. He tied orange and

21

black crepe paper bows on them and showed her the tattoo of Eeyore on his forearm. He told his friend he'd been having sex alone for so long it seemed almost wrong to involve someone else and laughed, and she knew he knew she'd heard him. She poured the Johnny Walker Black down her throat and felt it scorch, felt the inside of her mouth sparkle.

"What do you call a musician without a girlfriend?" he asked her.

"I don't know, what?"

"Homeless!"

Her own friends melted away and he went back to her place to make omelets—he said he used to be a short-order cook. On the walk by the lake under the Halloween stars he lent her his soft, thick sweatshirt and she knew she would give it back to him with the inside full of gold.

She knew it wouldn't last. She knew he could only be the Devil on Halloween night.

She was sure of this when he said "You're my angel" in her kitchen.

"Tonight," she said.

"Every night," he said. She knew he meant it at the time. Still, she hoped someday with someone to not know.

"You can't stay here," she kept saying after he kissed her. He did it on the cheek the first couple of times.

"No, no," he breathed and shook his head, with his brow furrowed, so serious. Elizabeth thought what a nice thing hard liquor was.

He went down on his knees in front of her, at her feet. His eyes were full of tears. They weren't flowing, not yet, not streaking down his cheeks, but they shone across his irises. He begged. "Let me stay, just let me stay, we can kiss all night." He looked at her, shaking his head the whole time.

She said, "It's not that I'm afraid of you," because she didn't want him to think that she didn't trust him, that she believed he might hurt her. He shook his head so fast when she said that.

"No," he mouthed, barely any sound coming out. "Oh, no."

"I don't know what I want," she said.

"It's been so long, it's been so long," he said. "Since I held anyone and kissed them all night. That's all we'll do. That's all we'll do." He nodded.

"This is your room?" Vinnie cried, not loud enough to wake her roommates, as he looked out her windows at the emerald trees rubbing and rustling against each other. Elizabeth's room used to be a sun porch. They could see the moon.

"Do you have any candles?" he asked.

"I think so," she said. While she was in the bathroom he set them up in twisted bits of foil. Her room was a Chinese lantern, red and flickering, and they were inside it. He was limber; he twisted both himself and Elizabeth around every which way.

"I need you to be gentler," she said.

"I'm sorry, I'm sorry," he said.

"I don't think you know how strong you are," she said, and he shook his head bashfully. She thought he blushed. His skin was very smooth, and pale, like a little boy's, but beneath it the muscles were hard against her fingertips.

Hours later he was still tumbling her around so much, and she was getting so content and sleepy. She just wanted to, was all.

She asked. "Do you want to make love to me?" she whispered. He heard her but he didn't give her an answer. He found the gold ring in her belly button and laughed. "Can I play with it?" he asked. He sounded delighted. His horns were askew and she took them off while she smoothed his hair.

His shoulders seemed massive when he rose up in front of her. Forever after she remembered them outlined in the windows, first against dark blue, then against white gray as the sky grew pale, grew light, grew dawn, grew morning. The way he moved was like a river, a wave, pushing his sparkling gold seeds up inside of her, back inside of her, and she had heard somewhere that men do this, push and push to get back in, full of regret that they ever left. So she moved toward him, and away from him, and toward him, and away from him, and in going toward him she was also going away from him, and maybe he was doing the same. He glowed almost blue and incandescent when his shoulders were framed by the gray and the fading stars. And Elizabeth was made of gold, and he sparkled, too, his face smeared with gold grains, his shoulders broad, spreading against the sky until he finally fell on her ribs.

❊ ❊ ❊

And now the gold glitter is everywhere, in Elizabeth's teeth, in her towels, in her sheets and pillowcases even though she washed them after he left. A single grain of it showed up in her pressed powder blush. It's on the collars of coats she hasn't even worn and winking at her from the grout between the tiles on the bathroom floor, impossible to get out no matter how many times she mops over the weeks and months. It's in her brushes, in her hair, in her lungs, on her tongue, in her belly, on her lawn, in her food, under her table. Floating on the surface of the lake. Everywhere.

Veronica

Ronnie got nightmares Good Friday night, everybody did. The Crucifixion, the stations of the cross, mass all afternoon in the auditorium, it was totally gross. Kelly Regan, everyone's favorite senior, called to participate, playing her guitar, accompanying an interpretive poem of some kind, intoning, "My Lord, what is Crucifixion? They put your hand upon the wood . . ."

Upon, thought Ronnie, *upon*, you can't just say *on*? Kelly had been irritating since Saint Ita's Elementary.

"They put your hand upon the wood, and pierce your flesh with the nail. It cuts through you. They raise the hammer high. The pain explodes"—special emphasis on *explodes*—"through your hand."

And Deirdre next to Ronnie draws in her breath and puts her face in her hands. The nail the nail the nail. They don't get the day off like the girls at Saint Scholastica, no, they get mass at school instead. That's how it is at Immaculate Conception. Immaculate Conception, one of the names of Mary, which does not, Sister Veronica the religion teacher said, have anything to do with Mary conceiving Jesus without having sex. Nothing at all.

"Mary, you must understand, was the one human being on earth who never sinned," said Sister Veronica. Sister Veronica was very old and it was totally weird to have to listen to her in religion class for honors sophomores on Catholic family life, which was the required curriculum. "Mary did not even carry the stain of

27

original sin. You understand, girls? Everyone else carries this sin, this vestige of the sins of Adam and Eve. But Mary, alone among all men and women, was chosen by God to be free of this burden. So that she would be worthy to carry Jesus. As the vessel. You see? Her conception, conception as a noun, girls"—not a trace of embarrassment as the girls squirmed, oh the misery of hearing a nun say "conception" although at least it was not as bad as hearing one say "intercourse"—"herself *as* a conception, she was conceived without sin. When we are conceived, we already carry original sin. She did not. She herself was a conception that was immaculate. The Virgin Birth is something altogether different."

Sister Veronica. Totally creepy to have the same name as the religion teacher nun, although of course nobody called Ronnie by that name, she was always just Ronnie. "I don't believe I don't believe I don't believe," Ronnie muttered under her breath all through class Good Friday morning before mass.

Dope with Julie Corbin and Deirdre that morning, too, in the bathroom, quick, but then the munchies and the attack on the vending machines in the cafeteria. They were sophomores, they were allowed to spend study hall in there as long as they kept up a B-minus average. But the day still dragged by, grueling and hot, an April heat wave.

Too old, oh too old for coloring Easter eggs in the arts and crafts room, for decorating candles with the Greek letters alpha and omega in religion class, the innocent preparations for the feast day to come. Ronnie was fifteen, school meant only the plaid skirt for her now. She wore gold chains with charms around her neck, that was her thing, all the girls had a thing. God, the things the girls wear! Whatever limits are put upon them, the white blouses, the vests buttoned, teenage girls will always find methods of adornment. The public school kids think they can't wear makeup but the nuns gave up on that long ago, in their mothers' time. Blue eye shadow was all the rage this year. Glitter makeup and socks with multicolored bright separate toes.

The thrill for the girls before the bell rang was Billy Joel

singing on their transistor radios in the hallway, "Come out, Virginia, don't let me wait, you Catholic girls start much too late."
Sometimes they did the Time Warp. They got to school in jeans
and then, at their lockers, pulled their plaid skirts up over them
and took the jeans off under their skirts. It meant demerits to get
caught with jeans in the building, but only Sister Mary Alice
really gave them. The other nuns pretended not to see.

※ ※ ※

The stations of the cross. Christ fell twice. There was no mention
in the Bible of anyone named Veronica wiping his face with her
head scarf out of mercy and finding his picture imprinted there
afterward, but there it was, that first stumble, intoned at station
six. That's not in the Gospels, Sister Veronica said in religion
class. "It's what is called a 'legend,' introduced into the story of
the road to Calvary by medieval Franciscans. Saint Veronica,
vera, true, and *icon*, image, true image, you see. Many of the
saints are now considered, since Vatican II, to be legends." Sister
Veronica lowered her voice to a whisper. "But girls," she said,
smiling wickedly, "I liked it better the other way."

Sister Veronica was getting forgetful. "Did we pray?" she
sometimes said halfway through class, when they had indeed all
said their Hail Mary in the name of the Father, and of the Son,
and of the Holy Spirit at the beginning, right after the bell. Sister
Veronica knew more names for the Virgin Mary than any nun or
priest Ronnie had ever known, and she used a different one every
day to round off the Hail Mary. Our Lady Seat of Wisdom, pray
for us, Our Lady Queen of Heaven, pray for us, Our Lady of the
Sacred Heart, pray for us, Our Lady of Sorrows, pray for us,
Blessed Virgin, pray for us, Mother of God, pray for us, Queen of
Angels, pray for us.

Ronnie sometimes wondered if Sister Veronica was going to
get in trouble one of these days because she often said little
things like she had said about the saints and angels, lowering her
voice and confessing to them that she liked things better the old

way. She had liked mass in Latin. She had liked the enforced silence and the reading of devotional texts at meals. She had liked wearing a habit—which she still did, alone of all the sisters of the Blessed Virgin Mary at Immaculate Conception. BVMs, Black-Veiled Monsters, the girls called them. As girls had since time immemorial, as Ronnie's and Deirdre's and Julie's mothers had, too.

So Saint Agnes without her eyes and Saint Agatha without her breasts were legends, and so was Saint Veronica. Like I care, thought Ronnie. Although, when Christ fell the first time, at the sixth station of the cross, at Good Friday mass, she got a quick picture of a Middle Eastern woman, a belly dancer, a veil across her nose and mouth, a flash of tribal bracelet at her wrist as she reached out with the cloth. The exact opposite of Sister Veronica.

"Chastity is a passionate vow, a passionate way of life," said Sister Veronica. "You must understand, girls. It opens so many doors for you."

All through mass Ronnie thought about It.

*   *   *

"I don't believe," Ronnie said, doing coke in Julie's basement on Saturday. The coke they bought from her older brother Quinn, who was in college at Loyola. Julie's parents were at mass. Mrs. Corbin was pretty into it. She went Saturday afternoon and Sunday morning, and Easter weekend Mr. Corbin went, too, but Julie hadn't been to confession yet. She had deliberately screwed up, not getting home from school soon enough Friday. God, the coke felt good. Coke is so good, so good, thought Veronica. It made her not think about It. They put on the *Rocky Horror Picture Show* soundtrack and did the Time Warp.

"Well, it's a pelvic thrust that starts to drive you insa-a-a-a-ane." Let's do the Time Warp again again again again again the nail the nail the nail the nail.

*   *   *

"Oh, *Mother!*" she said. "Do I *have* to?" Ronnie's mother had just told her to iron her dress for church.

"Yes, it's too wrinkled. It wouldn't get like that if you didn't stuff your closet like that and you cleaned it out like a clean, decent girl," her mother called from the living room to the kitchen, where the ironing board was.

Veronica was getting morning coffee for her mother, who was waking up there on the couch, which was It, the thing Ronnie thought about a lot, her mother sleeping every night on the couch. No pretense anymore. Wouldn't sleep with her father. Mouth open, sprawling on the fake brown suede cushions, quite a display. Ronnie didn't have Julie over anymore, her mom left the bedsheets on the couch as though she was almost proud of it, liked to rub Ronnie's nose in it. And Daddy was never home anyway, for Chrissake, she might as well have slept in the bedroom.

Ronnie wouldn't have had Julie or Deirdre at her house anymore anyway, not since her mother had yelled so loudly at her turned back that Julie had run out the front door. Well, Ronnie hadn't folded the laundry, that was true. And she had given her mom lip. Well, she was coked up, she gave more lip when she was coked up. But Mom could have waited till Julie left to yell at her like that, for Chrissake. "You think it's silly, dontcha? You think all this laundry and housework is silly, dontcha, that you're all above it, missy? Well, let me tell you, missy, when you're all alone and on your own and no one to do it for you, you'll think differently! Missy! Missy Too Good!"

Maybe she was mad because Ronnie, being only fifteen, did not have the misfortune of a husband who was fucking around. All Ronnie could figure out from her mother's anger was that it must seem terribly unfair to her, that her mother must be very upset that she should have to suffer something that her daughter did not. So that while Ronnie's friends got horrified imagining their parents doing it, Ronnie with horror could visualize her parents doing it and then not doing it. Oh, it doesn't matter, it doesn't matter, thought Ronnie, I don't care, I don't talk to my mother very much anymore anyway.

So, Sunday morning. Daddy silent, faceless, in the bedroom. He slept at home the night before because this morning was Easter. He'd done the same thing Christmas Eve. Ronnie was all dressed in powder blue and ironed and up while he hid in there, coming out just in time to drive them to Saint Michael's, where all the purple curtains were off the statues.

"They have taken away my master, and I know not where," Father Eustace intoned. Ronnie had confessed to him Saturday morning—been disrespectful to her mother three times, sworn twice. Nowadays she even threw in a few impure thoughts. Damned if she'd tell him about the coke. Or Tommy Dubovics. Which meant she wasn't in a state of grace, shouldn't have taken Communion. But she did anyway. "I don't believe, I don't believe," she muttered.

Bad guitar and off-key singing. "Christ has died alleluia Christ is risen alleluia Christ will come again alleluia alleluia."

There was Sister Veronica. Ronnie wondered why she wasn't at the chapel in the convent. She sat alone, there, in her habit. Father Eustace said "Go in peace," and while mass broke up and all the adults headed to the basement for the Easter morning coffee and cake celebration, Ronnie in her pale blue dress and headband and pastel pumps, one set of toes turned in as she stood, slipped from between her parents to see why Sister was there. For Chrissake, were they going to be overrunning her own church now, too? At first she didn't want to get too close but the nun saw her, and then she bowed her head shyly and said, "Hello, Sister. I didn't know you came here. Why didn't you go at the convent?"

"Oh, I went to the service at the chapel that was at sunrise. I thought it might help me to come to this one, too." Nuns nowadays could go where they pleased. Sister Veronica looked at Ronnie and while she did not smile she did not look mean, either. She also looked smaller than she did at Immaculate Conception.

Funny how different people look when you see them outside of where they usually are, Ronnie thought.

Then Sister Veronica did smile. "Ronnie!" she said with sudden recognition. "Of course. How nice to see you, to see another Veronica."

"Yes, Sister?" Oh, Sister was really losing it now.

"It's a good thing to be a Veronica," she said. "It is *we* who wiped his brow when he fell carrying his cross, and found the imprint of his face on the cloth. No matter what any man says. You know in bullfighting in Spain there is a motion of the cape called a Veronica, because it looks as though the bullfighter is wiping the face of the bull with his cape."

Ronnie looked at Sister Veronica from lowered, horizontal brows. That was interesting, if it was true.

"You should tell us about that stuff in religion."

"Another year, perhaps. We may get to religious symbols with Thomas Aquinas next year. If I am still teaching then." Her face was like a walnut.

"Sister?"

"Yes?"

"Is it really passionate?"

"Passionate?"

"You said . . . you said it was passionate to live the way . . . the way you do."

"Well, not passionate so much . . . you must remember, my dear, it was the only way then. . . . You know, you look quite different outside of school, quite grown up."

"It's the shoes."

"You look very pretty."

"Thank you, Sister." She looked expectant and Sister Veronica looked at her as though she wondered what she was expecting. "Yes? What is it, dear?"

"You said, 'It was the only way then'? The only way what?"

"Oh. Yes. Girls your age nowadays, they don't understand. The only way to go to college, to learn something, to teach, to be a doctor or a nurse or a writer. If you were a nun. You could travel. You could read and read and read."

"But is it fun?"

Sister Veronica considered.

"Think about living with all your girlfriends, with Julie and . . . and . . ."

"Deirdre O'Rourke."

"Yes. Living with them and talking with them or just being quiet with them all the time. Eating together and not caring about losing weight. No men around. No boys. Reading and staying up late, but getting up early, too, and thinking. It's like that."

"I don't believe," Ronnie burst out.

She expected anger but there was none. Only a calm "Why not, dear?"

"Because—do you remember when you were telling us, on Friday? That it wasn't easy for Jesus, that he felt pain, too, and was afraid, and he said, 'Lord, if it be at all possible, let this cup passeth from me? But be it done according to your will, and not to mine'? Because you wanted to show us how much he really suffered?"

Patiently. "Yes."

"But God didn't answer him."

"Ah. I see."

"That story, it's not like every other story I've ever heard about anything. In every other story, the point is to, you know, get the person to be all humble and ask, and as soon as they get the strength to ask and turn everything over to God, everything's okay. But God didn't answer him."

"No. God didn't answer him."

"Right."

"So you think that God is cruel, Veronica?" Such quiet inquiry.

"Yes, I do, Sister. How could he leave him there all alone?" What she was saying and who she was saying it to was finally sinking into Ronnie and she was suddenly afraid, very afraid. What would Sister Veronica do to her Monday morning?

"I will tell you a secret, Veronica," said Sister. "It is something we had best keep between ourselves."

Ronnie was trembling and looking down at her white tights, at that toe turned inward. Her hands were behind her back, her hair smooth beneath its pale blue headband. Her white lace collar belied, of course, that she had already done it twice with Tommy Dubovics in his cousin's van behind the Osco Market. Poor Tommy Dubovics, who, Ronnie suspected, got hit by his father *a lot*, more than the rest of them, more than she and Julie and Julie's brother and all the little O'Rourkes got hit.

And Sister Veronica lowered her dusty voice and said, "I sometimes think that God is cruel, too," and Ronnie could feel the cold despair in her breath and suddenly wanted to throw her arms around her to make her feel better. But then Sister Veronica beat her to it, held her tight, and she was surprisingly warm and soft for such an old woman, and Ronnie started to cry, and Sister Veronica whispered into Ronnie's hair, "It's all right, dear, it'll all be all right."

Snakes

I watch the black-haired jeweler at the Halloween fair pound out his silver rings on the anvil, chiming out the most simple rhythm, one two three four one two three four. His own fingers are circled with his handiwork, thick shining circles and squares. Geometric, masculine rings, tarnished black in checkerboards and crosses. My father was a jeweler, deep in the nineteen seventies. He and my mother owned a store, fragrant with incense, full of hoop earrings, beaten brass bracelets, peace signs. Hence my name, also from deep in the nineteen seventies. Peace.

The sky is the sapphire blue of October. Beneath it the stacked bales of hay shine gold, paid for by the merchants' association to give the block that harvest glow, and kids run around in the man-made, vine-decorated pumpkin patch, choosing their jack-o'-lanterns to be. All this, and the smell of pumpkin pie in the breeze. I can't eat pumpkin pie—nothing with too much shortening or butter in it—and I can't eat the barbecue, the scent of which is wafting on the air, either. White rice only, the doctor said. And clear broth and clear juice and if I really feel better, a banana. Rice cakes are okay, too. And instant oatmeal. My body is acting up again, my intestines curling around each other, twisting and cramping and swelling hard as stone.

The jeweler's hair is close and cropped, black like the night, or like the costumes the skeletons are wearing, the members of the merchants' association who are gamboling about the pumpkin patch frightening the children. The bones are painted white on their unitards and their faces are covered with masks like skulls. They're disjointed and jumpy, leaping around. They really should have thought of something more benign, like scarecrows. Some of the younger kids are starting to cry.

The jeweler's pet is a thick pale green snake, wrapped around his shoulders like a stole. Sometimes it pokes its head in his shirt pocket. The older kids gather around it and call "Eeeew!" and this makes the jeweler smile, though neither his eyes nor his hammer stray from his anvil. It makes me remember.

*　*　*

Nixon was reelected. As Watergate followed his fractured, paranoid soul into the White House and the denials and accusations and sound bites became ever more frequent, my mother simply had to leave the room when the news was on. There were things on TV that my mother couldn't watch. She just *couldn't stand* that voice, she said, that man was evil, evil, and on top of everything a Capricorn. And she couldn't watch *Jesus Christ Superstar* when it aired on Good Friday night, although I liked the overblown orchestral music. Hosanna, Heysanna, Sanna, Sanna Ho. There was unfortunately that scene where he is flogged by the Romans. My mother didn't approve of violence on television in any case and "I don't like it when they're mean to Jesus," she said sadly. Even if she was no longer a Catholic, even if she had married a Jew and raised her daughter in Christmas-present-and-Easter-basket-only American secularism.

She couldn't watch *Sesame Street*, either. The little one-minute movie of the snake hissing to teach the letter "S" made her cry out, "Oh, turn it off, turn it off!" because it would show up in the middle of the program with no warning.

My parents took me to Maine late that summer, before school started. I was eight. It was the one and only long-distance vacation we ever took, and I never did remember what had occasioned it. Perhaps some attempt to act like the parents of my friends at school? I didn't know. But I loved the idea. It was so much like the things my friends' families did in the summer. True, my parents didn't swim or sail or play tennis like the other parents, but this time I didn't even care. *I* swam. *I* rode the waves in the ocean, waves that knocked me down and buried me before I had a chance to hold my breath and filled my mouth with sand and salt. My father said that if I stood parallel to them I wouldn't get knocked down, but I liked the power of the sea, the feeling as the water slammed into my legs and tossed me in the air and then pulled me down, swallowing me. I loved the moment of being suspended in the wave, my arms and legs swirling around me like propellers but never hitting anything. And I always came up okay. I wasn't scared.

Sometimes, to get money for soda, I would go over to where my parents were reclining, in street clothes, on the beach. My mother, her long, thin body covered in mirror cloth pants and a white cotton peasant shirt, would be curled up on a beach chair, dozing. Her pale skin was slathered with total sunblock, of which there was only one brand in those days. I was careful running up to her because of the time she'd yelled, "My face is stinging—stinging right now! You need to be more considerate, young lady, more considerate of your fellow human beings!" when my feet had stirred whirlwinds of sand. My father lay with his book on his face, quiet and out of the way. He sketched designs for rings and pendants in pencil on a yellow pad. I sketched one, too.

"Will you make me that, Daddy?" It was a bracelet formed of letters that spelled out my name, P-E-A-C-E, Peace.

"When we get home," he said.

On the fourth day we didn't go to the beach. My mother wanted to see a Franciscan monastery that was about forty miles from where we were staying. The grounds were supposed to be beautiful, green and flowering, and she loved trees and flowers and nature. She often told us that, me and my father. She didn't like the city, she said. She didn't like our apartment, with only the concrete sidewalk in front of the building. When I got older I realized that places like this monastery dotted the Eastern seaboard; old, pretty religious houses run by Franciscans or Benedictines or Dominicans who charged a little toward their upkeep to let tourists wander the grounds and sometimes sold their specialties of wine or cheese or fruitcake.

My father drove us out that morning. My mother didn't drive. "The cars are all coming right at me," she said. "I have bad depth perception. It's not that uncommon." Whenever so much as a bicycle got within a few feet of the van, she grabbed my father's arm and took in her breath sharply.

But we got to the monastery just fine, paid a few dollars at the gate, and parked. There were bright gravel hiking trails and a little, dark hundred-year-old chapel with a statue of Saint Francis and short, fat candles for lighting. We started down one of the trails, which, like all of them, was crowded with tourists in shorts and T-shirts. I was behind my parents, and all of a sudden my mother just stopped.

I waited. I thought she would start walking again in a minute. But then I realized she wouldn't.

"What is it, Mom?" I asked, stepping up alongside her. But my father motioned me to be quiet and my mother's arm darted out to clutch me, so I stood still, too.

"What is it?" I whispered.

"Shh . . . be quiet!" hissed my father. Then I saw the little garter snake, the width of a pencil, sliding across the gravel like an emerald ribbon.

"What?" I asked again. I knew my mother didn't like snakes but I didn't understand *this*, I didn't know what it was.

I said to my mother, "Come on, Mama, it's okay. It's only a garter snake."

My mother's fingernails dug into my arm. She turned on me. "How do you know that? You don't know that!" she spat, loudly, so that some of the other people on the path turned to look at us. I longed to pull her arm away so it wouldn't be so obvious I was this woman's daughter. But my arm was the only thing that held my mother up and it was clutched with hot, iron fingers. My mother's mouth was set in the straightest line I had ever seen, the muscles tight and twitching, and I thought how much that must hurt. Later that day, back at the hotel, I looked in the mirror to see if I could ever make my face like that and my jaws and cheeks ached when I tried. My mother's eyes darted around and her chest rose and fell.

"Daddy," I said. Just "Daddy."

"Okay," he said. "Peace, we're going to turn and walk the other way now. Slowly. Don't let go of your mother." Couldn't he tell that I couldn't let go of her, that my mother had a hold on me and not the other way around? Didn't he see how white my arm was getting under her grip?

It took a couple of minutes to accomplish turning my mother around. Her face, usually ivory, was flushed and she had trouble breathing. Her feet moved only an inch off the ground as she stepped, as though she was afraid the snake would slither underneath them and surprise her. But she must still be able to walk, I thought. It was just a snake.

It was a little easier getting her down the gray-white path once she had turned her back on where the snake had been. When we got a few hundred feet away from the place, she drew her fingernails from my arm but she still clutched my wrist for support and twice she stumbled like a great stork and nearly fell, crying "Oh!" in a high, whinnying voice each time. It was still slow going. She relaxed more when we got onto the asphalt that led to the parking lot. I wondered if snakes were less likely to slide onto the pavement. We were almost at the van when my mother saw the dark wooden chapel, and she motioned toward it.

"Would you like to go in there?" my father asked. She nodded. He sighed one of his long, deep sighs. He took her arm then and he and I led her into the chapel.

There were some candles burning to a creamy statue of Saint Francis. My mother said she wanted to light one. I had never seen anyone light a candle to a saint and didn't know how it worked.

My mother took the change my father handed her and stumbled around confusedly. I wanted her to stop stumbling. I wanted to do whatever it was my mother wanted me to do for her so that we could leave this dark, cramped room and get back to the hotel and the beach, where I could leave her on a lounge chair and go off into the waves. But I didn't know how to help her. I didn't know what she was looking for. My mother's eyes were extra-wide like a baby's and blinking rapidly.

"What is it, lady?" said a man sitting in a dark corner of the chapel. I jumped because I had thought he was a bundle of something, maybe a giant sack of more candles. He was dumpy and dressed in a brown robe and rope belt. His voice was harsh and crude, not like I had always thought a priest or a monk would sound.

"I couldn't find a slot for the—" my mother began.

"Here, what is it, lady?" he broke in. He looked at her long patchwork skirt, her sandals and snowy white, bony ankles beneath it, my father's red beard. "Do you want to light a candle? There, look, there's the place for the money, no, for goodness sake, *there*, lady, right in front of you." Finally the monk shuffled over to her, took the coins from her hand, and put them in a slot in the box attached to the wooden railing in front of the statue. Then he walked out of the chapel, shaking his head.

"Oh, now he made me feel bad. He made me not want to light one," she said. She was blinking rapidly again. Three or four more people had come in when the monk went out and I knew they could hear her, so I wanted to hurry things along. My father sighed deeply again.

"Well, I think if you want to light one, you should light one," I said. "Want me to do it for you?" I stretched out my hand and saw the crescent-shaped welts from her fingernails on my arm. I hadn't looked at them before. They fascinated me, the way it fascinated me and my schoolmates to weave pins in and out of the top layers of the skin on our fingertips.

My mother shook her head. Her hand was trembling, so it

took a while but finally she managed to light a candle in the blaze of the ones that were already burning away, and she put it on one of the spikes in front of Francis, who was all a-flutter with baby sparrows lighting on his hands and a doe and tiny squirrels and other woodland creatures around his feet, like Disney's Snow White. For a few minutes she gazed quietly into the flame.

I watched her, watched her lower lip tremble, and that was the instant I knew that there was something inside me like a box. A metal box, deeply, deeply buried beneath the flesh, suspended in my insides beneath my stomach behind the muscle wall. It had sharp corners and it poked, and I felt I could take nothing else inside myself but what went in this box. So I put this, this thing that was happening for real in front of me, my mother lighting a candle to Saint Francis—he used to be her favorite saint, she had told me sometimes at home—I put it in the box. Or it dove in of its own accord, the opposite of what all the different terrors in Pandora's box had done. I supposed there would be other things in there, too. Even then I knew.

We went home to the city, and in a few weeks the cold gray autumn closed in around us. I preferred autumn.

⁂

It lurks now, always. Ripping my guts to shreds. I am very thin, I never do take much in. But there is nothing wrong with me. They have tested for everything. No cancer, no growth, no parasite. Only the cold metal box that the lower GI does not detect.

"Can I hold him?" I ask. I motion to the snake.

"Sure. Be gentle with him, though. He spooks easy." The jeweler takes him off like a scarf, with both hands, holds him out to me, and I reach for him. I put him against my cheek. The skin. It's smooth and dry, as though covered with a thousand tiny mirrors, like the Indian cloth I remember my mother's dresses were made of. It curls around my shoulders and pokes its little head down my back, under my shirt, into my front jeans pocket.

I know that the world can be very hard on some people, tor-

ment them with the poverty of Great Depressions and the terrors of great wars, frighten them with the ravings of drunkards or
the harshness of those who should love them most. Leave them
hopelessly damaged and unable to grow up inside, cut in two
from just plain sensitive natures and bad luck and inability to
thrive. I know in my heart that my mother was one of these. But
oh, how defiant I feel, how strong, stroking the python as it glints
in the setting sun.

"Make me a snake?" I say to the jeweler. His eyes are gigantic
and dark beneath the cropped hair.

"Sure. Ring, bracelet, what?"

"Not to wear. Just a snake."

The night is falling. Jack-o'-lanterns from the pumpkin patch
gleam.

"You'll miss the prizes for the costumes."

"I don't mind."

"Okay."

He takes out a lump of silver, places it on the anvil, raises his
hammer. The troupe of dancing skeletons closes in around us, to
watch. They make me laugh, wiggling and leaping so frantically.
The stroke of the hammer on the silver rings out over the street.

The Falling Nun

I hate that goddamned three-inch-high plastic nun I got out of the Archie McPhee mail-order catalog of silly toys. We all bought them, all the women in the office, as a joke, because of the silly things the catalog said about them. But I can't stand it now. I can't stand it.

◦ ◦ ◦

The first time Tom kissed me it went on and on and he ran his tongue over my bottom lip and I thought, "I don't care if I never see him again, that was the best kiss I've ever had. I'm happy with just that kiss." Now, I know that was no more true than it sounds but it was a romantic thought, and now, now that my nuns have done their work, now that I sit here in the office, I can let myself know that he won't kiss me again.

Thank God the chair I'm sitting in is hard. If it were soft it would be too easy to think, and I don't want to think. I've got a headache, too, and thank God for that. Maybe he is looking out for me, after all. I thought the nuns would be more benevolent toward me, because they were women. True, they were not entirely like the rest of us, they were eternally virgins and so would know nothing about the love of men, but some women might become nuns because of disappointed love, and that would give them some empathy. And there is such a thing as sisterhood, isn't there? They would understand, they would help, they wouldn't betray me. But maybe that was bullshit. Maybe I do crave God, a man after all, to help me.

* * *

It was Tom's beauty that attracted me to him, his beauty alone, not his personality or his mind. I could be as shallow as any man, to begin with. I didn't care at first about his alcoholic, wife-beating father or his cowering mother or his wounded soul. I still don't, I don't think. Does that make me a lot like a man? He became too much for me, too much for me to be patient with.

Oh, I don't know, maybe I do care about his wounded soul, after all. But fuck him.

* * *

Here is the deal with the nuns. There is this catalog out of Seattle, trendy, the thing everyone wants to say they knew about before it became mainstream. The company that puts it out is called Archie McPhee, after some legendary guy who knew how to have fun, and it sells kitsch and campy remembrances of twentysomething and baby-boomer childhoods—Jetsons dolls, lawn flamingos, whatever they can find. They buy out old lots of useless but cool stuff and people like me and my friends eat it up. And they advertised these nuns, five per cellophane pack, on the same page as some other religious paraphernalia. They were for decorating First Communion cakes or something, I don't know.

I remember from my World Mythology class in college that in almost all religions the moon and the night are feminine, governed by the long rhythms thought to be female, represented by goddesses—Diana, Luna, and that weird one from Egypt, Nut. Nut held herself up on her hands and feet and stretched over the earth so that she *was* the night sky. The night as the living body of a woman. Mysterious, aloof, and beautiful.

Now, this is all very flattering. But some male high priest made it up, you could tell. If a woman had made up the mythology, the night would be the living, breathing body of a man, held up by his broad shoulders, moving slowly and eternally above her, covered with stars.

＊ ＊ ＊

I will *not* call him. I will not call him to tell him our quasi-romance is over after he has gone for three weeks without calling me. I won't do it, I am too ashamed to even let him know I noticed. My God, am I just like everybody else? Everybody who has ever been obsessed with someone they want more than the someone wants them? Do we all circle forever in never-ending, miserable spasms of this feeling, in constant wishes that another person is thinking, talking, wondering about us? Do we never outgrow it? And if not, what the hell are we supposed to do?

＊ ＊ ＊

In the Archie McPhee catalog they print letters from their customers, from loyal fans in on the joke. One woman sent a letter that said that she had ordered the set of five tiny, hollow plastic nuns and put them on top of the partition of her cubicle. She hadn't had a date in two years. And one day she arrived at her cubicle to find that one of the nuns had fallen to the ground. That very day, someone asked her out.

After that the letters came thick and fast. Apparently these nuns often had this effect. Falling nuns equaled auspicious events in love lives, usually those of women. Well, sometimes they meant other things. There were letters from travelers who had, instead of getting dates, run into nuns who needed rides back to their convents. Letters from computer hackers who had hit upon perfect programs after nuns fell on them. But mostly it was women. And mostly the nuns brought men, men with dates and flowers, men who called when they said they would and remembered to ask about Saturday night before Friday morning. And so the women I work with and I—I work at a computer magazine, writing reviews of Mac products—we ordered a couple of cellophane packs. As a joke, God help us. We got one each. I put mine on the windowsill. I was lucky, my cubicle faced a window. She was so tiny, she wasn't even all that noticeable. There were pink lawn flamingos and a Bart Simpson planter full of hydrangeas there, too. And an Elvis tapestry instead of curtains.

The nuns were all identical: three inches high, in black habits with a touch of white around the veil. Youngish. Little round mouths, probably meant to look like they were singing in a choir. Features very prettily painted on, in pink and black and white. There were touches of gold on the rosaries that dangled on their habits, and they held open missals in their little hands.

* * *

I'm at the Mac now, in my hard little chair, with my headache. No one notices that I'm not typing a review. In a way I wish everyone were out of the office so I could call and hear his voice on his answering machine. And leave him a message, a mature message, that I wanted to talk, that it seemed something had happened but perhaps we were just misunderstanding each other. But I'm so, so glad there are too many people around for me to make a personal phone call, because that would be just too humiliating. How does this happen? It seems like the very act of feeling that way about someone makes it impossible that they can ever feel that way about you, because you can never want someone who obviously wants you. It's the rule of the playground. The rule of you like him, oh yes you do, I'm going to tell, Jane loves Dick, Dick loves Spot. Sitting in a tree, K-I-S-S-I-N-G. Or F-U-C-K-I-N-G. It's a juvenile rule. We all know that. But it's still the rule, and we play by it.

* * *

Tom has a sister named Grace. I never met her, but he told me about her. She was two years younger than he was and she had grown up among her henlike Irish aunts after his parents divorced, while he had lived with his abusive father and his mother was working nights nursing. I asked him once what she looked like. I guess I wanted to know if she was as beautiful as he was.

"She has really pretty red hair," he said. We were at my kitchen table, drinking tea after we'd been out together. It was our little ritual, the only one we had, so I prized it. "Really thick, really gorgeous hair. And very white skin and very blue eyes." He hesitated for a moment and took some of his tea. "She takes after my father's side of the family. He's really big, you know? Over six feet, and when he was drinking he would sometimes hit two eighty. So she takes after that side of the family."

I looked at the curves of the muscles of his thighs under his jeans, at the delicate way his back narrowed from his shoulders to his waist, at the spray of his hair that fell into his eyes. His little sister, then, was what is called, with such irritating euphemism, a "big girl." So he was the pretty one.

＊　＊　＊

When he took me to dinner after work, the waitresses, the hostesses—you can imagine. Most guys look a little emasculated in nice suits, dress shirts, ties. Not Tom. His arms, his legs, his back, they just shone through, moving under the fabric with so much confidence and strength and that form of grace that belongs only to men. I thought there was some kind of promise in the ease with which he moved, something still unrealized, some hint of an experience yet to come.

The time we went hiking for the day in Big Basin he told me a story about Grace. Actually he told it to me on the drive down, on winding roads through the green and yellow hills of Northern California. He said it was his favorite story about her, but it was sad.

He said it happened when he had just come back from Europe, where he had been wandering around, doing the starving student thing. He had a girlfriend back home whom he was writing to while he was there and he hooked up with another girl in England and he kept them both going simultaneously. Any-

way, he was back home, sitting in the living room with the rem-
nants of his family, and somehow this came to light—someone
found a letter or something—and his aunts started clucking over
it. "That Tom," they said. "That rakish Tom and his exploits."

Tom shook his head when he told me about this and then he
said, "And my sister's tone of voice was exactly the same, I mean
indistinguishable from my aunts'. *Tom and his exploits. Oh, that
Tom.* I wanted to say to her, Come on, you're two years younger
than me, you should be having your own exploits." He was
driving, so he didn't look at me, he looked at the winding road.

I turned toward him a little from the passenger seat and
said, "I don't know. Exploits aren't for the faint of heart. It's just
that there are so many reasons for a person to end up faint of
heart."

"Well, don't misunderstand me, it's not that I want my sister
to be sleeping around," he said. "And she's not faint of heart."

"I didn't mean just that kind of exploit," I said. But I did. "And
I don't presume to know anything about your sister," I said. But I
did. No one would think I was faint of heart either, would they?
They wouldn't. But I am.

"But it's just . . . don't you think that's sad?" he insisted. He
looked at me, expecting something.

"I don't know," I said. "How could it have been different?"

"I guess it couldn't," he said slowly, and gave up. We were not
going to connect about this. I couldn't give him the thing that he
wanted.

He said he was pleased, though. He said Grace had a date Saturday night, which was unusual for her. How could I tell him
that before my nun and him it had been unusual for me, too?
How could I tell him that faced with tales of his exploits I would
have allied myself with a bunch of old Irish aunts, too, because it
would have been all I had?

I thought it was the saddest story in the world.

* * *

The last time Tom kissed me was six weeks ago, the night we got back from Big Basin. Six weeks.

My God, there was a time his hands ran over my thighs and I could not open my mouth wide enough to match his and I put my hand on his cheek and it was so smooth that as I pulled away I murmured, smiling, "You shaved this morning," and he said, "I shaved tonight," and he stopped and cast down his eyes and finished, "I thought we might be doing this, so . . ." and I laughed at him and pulled him toward me and his arms went so tight around me I couldn't breathe.

He went home not much later. He always went home.

* * *

We wrote poems about the nuns to each other at work on our e-mail:

> *My nun is still*
> *Eyes turned flirtatiously toward her missal*
> *Pretending to sing songs of purity*
> *Her silence, her steadfastness*
> *Will no finger tip her over?*
> *She mocks me.*

The day my nun fell over was the day Tom asked me out for the first time. But by now you know that. The only unexpected thing about it was that I thought one of my friends had knocked it over for a joke. But I asked everyone and they all said they hadn't.

I wrote:

> *Enough.*
> *She has fallen.*
> *What pale finger sent her toppling?*
> *What delicate hand caused her to be so upset?*
> *To which star-crossed fate*

Do I abandon myself
On my return home this evening?
Oh, why does she smirk at me,
Her little feet pointed toward the ceiling?
I wait.
I tremble.

                    ✦   ✿   ✦

Margaret's nun fell over two days after mine. Margaret is our
supervisor and has her own office. She had just broken up with
her boyfriend, and she kept her nun on her computer terminal.
Two days later an old friend who had always been sweet on her
called and they went to dinner.

                    ✦   ✿   ✦

Tom wasn't in his twenties anymore, he was thirty-four. I was
twenty-seven. Maybe that was what he liked about me, the
twenty in my age. I was still seeing him when I had my birthday,
when I turned twenty-eight. He brought me white roses. He
remembered those are my favorite kind, and I had only told him
once. And he gave me a Tom Waits CD. It was one he knew I
didn't have. I don't have a CD player, though, mine's blown and
I haven't gotten another one yet, I'm too poor. That he forgot.

                    ✦   ✿   ✦

My friend Lorelai was having an affair with the guy across the
hall from her in her apartment building. He was still living with
his bisexual girlfriend, but he said they weren't sleeping
together. He just came over to Lorelai's place whenever he felt
like it. She said she didn't care, she wasn't in love with him. But
she'd had a fight with him because he never asked her anywhere
or took her out, so he didn't show up for three weeks. She acci-
dentally knocked over her nun with a box of file folders and that
night he came over. He took her to see Nirvana and the Breeders
in a benefit for Bosnian rape victims.

Susan the accounting manager's Rollerblading buddy made a pass at her.

I am not making any of this up, you know.

◦   ◦   ◦

When we got back from Big Basin, Tom drove me home and I said, "So what would you like? Do you want to come in for a while or head home?" and he said he wanted to come in. We sat on my couch, and he started to kiss me, and that went on for a while. Then he toned down his kisses and said it was time for him to go home. This time, to get back at him because he wasn't trying to stay, I told him I was nervous and I wanted to take things slowly, would that be okay? He kissed my cheek and said, "Fine," and he has not kissed me one time since, except on the cheek, and he gives me only big brotherly bear hugs good-bye. I've tried to kiss him, thinking I might have made him shy. He would let me do it with a politeness that twisted my stomach, but he never responded. His mouth was yielding but passionless. How could he control himself like that? If he wanted to kiss me, how could he not do it? I couldn't do that, not in a million years. If I wanted to kiss someone, I would kiss him. Is that what being a man does? Can they really all cover things up like that, can they really control themselves so that anything tender goes someplace other than the heart, someplace like the left calf, and stays there so it doesn't affect the body? I don't know if I envy this or not.

◦   ◦   ◦

What catches in my head is how fast he said it when he told me, "My father is an alcoholic." How he was telling some story about his family and he started that sentence and then paused after "My father" and then raced past with the rest of it, so fast that if I hadn't been listening to him very carefully I wouldn't have caught it.

A poem:

I will smash my nun.
She tortures me
Although she is only plastic.
She giggles away silently
As silently as the phone.
If only I could send her back
To Archie McPhee, where she came from
But she is part of a set.
Still, I shall make her pay
For the havoc she has wrought.

I got a picture in my head while I wrote this to e-mail to Lorelai. A little muscle between my shoulder blades jerked as I looked up at my nun on the windowsill. In my wandering mind, I saw her take out a comb and, while her veil slipped from her head, comb out her long hair. I sat very straight in my chair. I wanted something solid and hard against my back.

* * *

The word "him." There is something about it, its warmth, its song. He fit it. I love that word. Maybe "her" has a magic for men. I don't know. But either way, what am I supposed to do? What am I supposed to do?

He didn't kiss me but still he called, still he asked me out, still he hugged me. I went when he asked. He told me personal things about himself sometimes. He had herpes but I was very nice when he told me and I said it didn't make any difference. That wasn't what he wanted to hear, somehow. It was something I had suspected, actually, a good-looking man like that who had slept with so many women. I had asked him why he was going so slowly and that was what he told me, that he had herpes—well, first he said we hadn't had a modern conversation about where we had been and who we had been with, and *then* he told me about the herpes, and I kissed him, but he pulled his mouth away and held me.

He didn't stop calling me until after we fell asleep on his couch.

* * *

We were going to watch TV, Tom and me, after a dinner party we went to, and we just fell asleep. We had had a lot of wine at dinner. Once I woke up and he asked what I was dreaming. I said, "There were two kids with fishing poles, and they wanted to come say hi to us where we were on the banks of a river, but they couldn't find a place to leave all their tackle. What were you dreaming?"

"I hardly ever dream," he said. "I could just tell by the way you were moving that you were."

He tangled his legs up with mine and we fell asleep again. He dozed off before I did, so I watched his beautiful face, his razor-sharp cheekbones and nose, his light brown hair, his chest rising and falling under his sweater. Maybe he only forgot his dreams— I read somewhere that everybody dreams many times every night, but that most of the visions are forgotten. Was he seeing his father in his sleep; his big, broad, drunken, handsome father who hit his mother and sister and him? Was he reliving his own exploits?

A few times he woke up and whispered "Hi" to me and I said "Hi" back and we fell asleep again, like lovers after the first time. He still hadn't kissed me, but I didn't even mind. He would again, I knew. It would be that night, I knew. He would kiss me before morning, I knew.

* * *

I was seeing nuns everywhere. I noticed them as extras in movies. They seemed to walk ahead of me in pairs on every street. They jutted out in front of me from the doors of Catholic schools, appeared in medieval paintings on postcards at museums I visited. I saw a very fat one in the park. She was like a big ship in her old-fashioned habit, one of those nuns who had to have a name like Sister Saint Cornelius. I overtook her. "Hello, Sister," I said.

She smiled, a hard, iron smile, but still a smile. She can't have been used to young women saying "Hello, Sister" to her in the park. "Hello," she said back at me, and walked on. Looking at her bulk, I was suddenly ashamed of the delicacy of my bones, of my young body.

*　*　*

Lorelai and I were working late. It was getting hard for me to concentrate because I was wondering what things meant when Tom did them. Do you know what I mean? Like why did he walk around without his shirt after he took a shower before we went out to dinner after we'd been at the beach and then not put his arm around me all night? Like what did it mean that he forgot where he parked the car the first three or four times he went out with me, so that we wandered for blocks, hand in hand, looking for his Jetta, but that the last time I saw him he told me after dinner that the car was two blocks down and over in front of the furniture store? And why, *why* did I so often turn around and catch him lifting his eyes guiltily from my cute little ass, where his hands never ventured to go?

Well?

"Did you hear that?" said Lorelai from her cubicle.

"What?"

"That." There was a little moaning, a tiny wail, like a puppy's, sliding through the halls.

"Maybe a dog in the alley," I said. But I wanted my back against something hard and solid again.

*　*　*

Tom suddenly squeezed my shoulders after we had been sleeping on his couch for hours and said, "I better take you home."

"You're not too tired?"

"No."

"Well, if you're not too tired, okay, but if you are, I can crash here and just go to sleep."

Oh, Holy Mary, Mother of God, how long it took him to say anything. How his eyes moved under their closed lids as he searched for insultingly diplomatic words.

"I think I'll do the gentlemanly thing and take you home," he finally said. How I hated him for it. As though I had asked him to do anything ungentlemanly. I was so careful to say, "and just go to sleep."

But when he opened his eyes, his brows were all knitted up and he looked as though he was afraid of something.

"Is that okay?" he asked.

"That's fine," I lied, running my fingers very gently over his chest, just once.

"Although," he said, "I mean, snuggling with you for most of the night sounds pretty great, but . . ."

"But what?" I said.

"What?"

It took everything I had and it scared me to do it, but I repeated what he had said. "You said snuggling with me for most of the night sounded pretty great, but . . . so, but what?"

"Oh, I do that. Sometimes I don't finish my sentences." And he got up and put on his shoes.

✳ ✳ ✳

I was just back from lunch, watering my hydrangeas. I picked up my nun. Before I knew what I was doing, I silently asked her to help me. I put her down carefully but she fell over on her side. Did that mean anything? If you did it with your own hand but it was truly an accident, did it mean something?

A couple of mornings ago, as we stood next to the coffee machine waiting for the pot to fill, Lorelai confessed to me, "I'm falling in love with him." Then she said, "Motherfucker."

"I'm so sorry," I said. Then, "Are you *sure* they're not sleeping together?"

"That's what he says," she said, and sighed. "Motherfucker."

She sent me an e-mail that afternoon.

Nuns, a haiku
Fuck that fucking nun
Fuck fuck fuck fuck fuck fuck fuck
I wish she were dead.

I wrote her back, "She's plastic. She is dead."
"I don't give a fuck," Lorelai wrote. "I want her really dead."

*   *   *

Tom tried hard on the way home. He was so careful. He put his hand on my knee, which was bare and smooth, because I always shaved my legs so carefully before I went out with him. He kept looking over at me. I held his hand where it lay and looked out through the window, not at him.

"Are you okay?" he asked when he pulled up in front of my building.

I nodded. "Why wouldn't I be okay?" I said. I looked around the car, getting my purse, my jacket. Encouraged by the hand that rested on my knee all through the drive home, I said, "I just want to kiss you," and then I did. I tried to be very soft, not make him think I expected him to slip his tongue into my mouth or bite the corner of my lip or grip my scalp through my hair, all of which he had once done, in a time that seemed much longer ago than it could really have been.

At first it was all right. For a second he opened his mouth a little and his hand touched my neck. And then he shut down, like a computer, and pulled away as soon as he had finished the mechanics of what he was doing, as soon as he could get his mouth pressed against mine and then release it.

"Good night," he said.
"Good night," I said.

*   *   *

When I was with him I slowly, surely turned toward his body, like a compass needle turned toward north, aching; but my own body apparently held no such tantalizing mystery for him. It didn't hide anything he wanted to uncover. Sometimes, though, I hear a nagging, brave little whisper in my head, like his tender fingers on the back of my neck (and God, they were light, so light), "Yes it did. *Yes it did.*"

I called him and left a message a few days later, and a few days after that. And he never returned the calls, and I knew somehow he wouldn't, and I kept my dignity and stopped calling. Nobody knew how hard that was. Nobody knew how my heart pounded when I dialed, my relief and disappointment at getting his machine. Nobody knew how I fought calling, thinking, "It's eleven-fifty; make it until noon," like a recovering alcoholic trying to make it through one day at a time, every ten minutes until it was too late at night to call.

Lorelai sent me an e-mail. She was listening to music in her cubicle and I yelled at her to turn it up, but the other people in the office shouted me down, so she sent me the lyrics. It was the Pogues, screaming away in their Irishness. Wailing banshees with combs in their hands, dead men's countries and damned souls.

Margaret found her nun facedown next to the filing cabinet. "How'd it get there?" she said, staring at it.

"Has it been like that long?" asked Lorelai.

"It's been missing for days," answered Margaret.

"You mean it could have been lying like that for *days?*" said Lorelai. "Pick it up, quick! Who knows what goddamn damage it's done already?"

"Tell me about it," said Margaret. She took the nun and went back to her office, her high heels and chignon looking oddly tough and hard.

I'm sitting here at the Mac, quietly letting go of him, trying to gently ease myself away. It's hard, but I know I can do it, I know I can. He does not want me, he cannot want me. He will never, ever kiss me again, I will never, ever feel his fingers on the back of my neck again, and I will never, ever understand why. Just one of those opaque reasons, something for him to keep private. Who knows what trauma, what irritation, what boredom I awoke in him? Who knows what his story is?

I think of his sister and I try to think of how she must feel, and maybe she feels even worse than I do. Think of how afraid she must be, how close she keeps her heart, I tell myself. Think how awful that must feel. At least I had something, I say to myself. At least once or twice I had some glimmer, some bright thread of a touch between me and another human being who, for a few seconds, maybe I loved, yeah, who knows, there's no way to tell now but maybe for a minute there I loved him, heaven help me, simply because he was in the same pain as all the rest of us.

Was I wrong, to love such a man? Did those great goddesses of the moon and the night, Isis, Diana, Nut, Aphrodite, scorn me for my weakness when faced with him? But isn't this love for men the most powerful and feminine force of all?

I say to Lorelai, over the cubicle partitions, "My nun is laughing at me. I could take it if she wouldn't fucking laugh."

"Mine is too," says Lorelai.

We stand up, as if on command. We both know what we're going to do. I walk with sure, definite steps to the windowsill, pick the nun up, throw her on the floor, stomp on her. She's made of awfully hard plastic and it takes a lot to break her.

Lorelai, beside me, is wearing her Doc Martens and she gives it a try, and she crushes her nun with a wonderful snap, and we both go to work on mine, and as we do it, little shrieks escape from the splitting plastic, like the voices of mice or tiny children.

Margaret comes out of her office to see what's going on and when she does see she goes back and returns with her nun and spikes her with her dress-for-success high heels, and soon the whole place, up and down the halls, private offices and cubicles, is filled with the wails of the tiny nuns as we all smash the motherfucking little bitches to kingdom come. Nothing can help us, you know. Nothing.

Bethlehem

Miranda. Can. Not. Stop. Crying. She has always cried a lot but this is beyond the beyond. She has no ability at all to regulate it. She has tried just letting herself have a good cry alone in her dorm room to get it over with but it doesn't help, it just adds to the sum total of tears. Anything sets it off, the most maudlin of crap, she watched *General Hospital* in the lounge and that did it this time. Those poor people. All those problems, never-ending, insoluble. And of course there was the news, with the shelters that didn't have enough toys from the holiday drive for the homeless kids. *It's a Wonderful Life.* Anything will do it. Everyone's life is pain.

She will have to call the student health center and tell them it's not working. The Zoloft was supposed to be totally effective by the end of week two but it is not working, *not working*, they will have to up the dose or switch her to Prozac. Look, she's still crying, she still can't stop, even in Walgreen's, where she went to get some milk for her dorm room instant morning coffee, even as she stands over the Christmas cards and the sets of lights and the ornaments and the dancing Santas and the blue Hanukkah tinsel and Star of David decorations and electric menorahs and the Kwaanza children's books. She's still crying. The psychiatrist they have at student health one day a week to dispense these drugs to the undergrads says that Zoloft for reasons unknown seems to work well with women, but prescribing these medicines is an art, not a science. Miranda hasn't slept in two nights, but is that the insomnia of what he has categorized as her clinical depression or is it from the drug she's taking to control it? The only way to know, said the psychiatrist, in his Birkenstocks, is to experiment with the dose. Well, she'll have to call them.

So. The music of the Walgreen's, the people all around her, make no difference. She can suppress her actual noise, though it causes a barely noticeable shuddering across her back. But maybe no one can see that. It's sunny outside even though it's cold, the kind of day Miranda used to enjoy before the full force of the unhappiness of the world so insidiously crept up upon her. Maybe the streaming tears don't show behind her sunglasses.

It's Friday well after five and she's on her way through campus now, Walgreen's behind her, to make up her astronomy lab. One lab science is required to graduate. History of Astronomy is the class of choice for the humanities students, the comp lit majors like Miranda. Not that she's read anything lately, the books all start the waterworks. The unjust, helpless execution at the end of *The Stranger*, Raskolnikov's miserable understanding of what he's done in *Crime and Punishment*, Sydney Carton's laying his life down for the husband of the woman he loves in *Tale of Two Cities* and comforting that poor seamstress on the way to the guillotine. Miranda liked the seamstress far better than the heroine who escaped with her life and her husband. How could they live, how can she live, in such a world as this? Everyone is miserable, everyone is wretched, everyone tries so hard for such modest dreams and doesn't get them. And Miranda is useless, she can't help anyone, she can't even stop crying.

She has to make up the lab, she has to, or she'll get an incomplete. Her room is a mess, she hasn't got time, she can't organize her thoughts enough to put her clothes away. It will have to stay just like that. So long past five, the health center is closed, and will not open again until Monday.

The psychiatrist tried to be kind. "How can anyone not be depressed nowadays?" he said to her. But that doesn't change anything. They're still not open until Monday. She'll have to get through until then.

Her dad was laid off at the optical shop. It was bought out by a LensCrafters. He's not a doctor, someone whose name the customers know, he just grinds the lenses and makes the glasses. There are many like him, unimportant, so they did not keep him on. Miranda is on so much financial aid here at school that she can probably continue, but her dad had wanted some little things. To save enough to open a music store, a store of imported Eastern European CDs. Her dad played guitar and bouzouki and balalaika, none of them all that well but he loved them. He wanted to be his own boss. He had done the research, he knew what he was doing. In that neighborhood, so full of recent immigrants, between Kedzie and Edsel, where he had his eye on the space, the store could do very well.

They would be okay, they wouldn't lose the little house. Miranda's father was no fool, he had savings. Savings for the imported music store. But now there would be no store.

Her father once told her the story of his own grandfather's restaurant, The Troika. His grandfather had planned for a shining grand opening on New Year's Eve, a party with musicians—an accomplished one himself, he would sing. Money was borrowed for the food, the equipment, to pay the chef. There was work for months to get it all ready—Miranda's father, only a little boy, had helped to paint and clean and unload the dishes as they arrived from their fresh, clean white boxes, layered with newspaper. The place was fully booked. But now there was a storm New Year's Eve and no one could make their reservation. It sat empty.

"They went broke their first night," said Miranda's father, smiling wryly.

"Oh, Daddy!" Miranda cried.

"It's okay, honey, it's okay," said her father. He considered her. "My mother was like that. If you said something just that way, she'd cry." He looked at her again, smiling, shook his head. "There's an old Russian joke," he said. "A lady says, 'On Christmas

Eve, I heard a knocking on my door, and I went to answer it. Oh, it was terrible, there was an old man there and a little girl, skin and bone, just starving, not a crust of bread to eat, it was so upsetting, it was terrible, in the end I just couldn't bear to look at them like that. So I had to shut the door.' " Now her father's smile was not wry. It was much softer. "My mother cried at that," he said, while Miranda's own eyes welled up with tears. He patted her head as he walked away, and he did not tell her either story again.

Miranda walks fast. She has to make up the lab. She will get an incomplete. She knows this from Ramon the TA. He doesn't actually teach the course—the professor does that—but he's in charge of the planetarium labs and making sure the reluctant students mark the right stars in their lab workbooks. Miranda stayed in her room the last lab, trying to have her good cry, trying to get it all out, figuring it was better that way, and then it would be over and she could go on from there, before she knew it wouldn't help. In a brief respite when her body was sore from being wracked by the sobs but otherwise quiet, she went to see Ramon as the period ended to ask if she could come to the makeup lab on the final day of class. "Sure," he said, clearly out of patience with her, with all the students who blew off their History of Astronomy labs. "But you really do have to make it up. You'll get an incomplete otherwise and I don't have any control over that." He didn't look at her. He was busy shutting down the console that controlled the movement of the stars, that ran the tapes in the planetarium. "You really do. Six on the twenty-first."

"Six in the morning?" Miranda's heart sank. Between five and seven seemed to be the only time she could sleep.

"Six at night. But be on time, I can't stay late because I've got telescope time that night."

Telescope time, for the real astronomy students, in the real observatory. Not for comp lit majors like Miranda.

Someone in lab once asked Ramon what the grad students did up there in the observatory all night. Ramon had long, long black hair and a black mustache and was very skinny. His round glasses were much too big. "You just hang out and watch *Star Trek* and crunch your numbers and wait for your time," he said mildly, pointing out the Pleiades with the lighted arrow that flew about the planetarium dome. *Star Trek.* So they really were all Trekkie nerds, as the humanities students suspected.

Miranda arrives at the Math and Sciences hall. The lights are dim inside the planetarium, but she keeps her sunglasses on to hide the tears. She can't keep her sniffles silent, but she coughs pointedly. People will think it's a cold. She wants to let herself go at least a little now so that she will have the strength left to clamp down during the actual lab program.

Six or eight students dot the seats. Miranda takes one, near Ramon's control panel, where the other students do not seem to congregate. She grits her teeth in preparation. The lights grow dimmer, slowly, except for the one over the console. She hears Ramon slide in a tape of some kind, hears the machinery accept it. Then another click as he starts a cassette player, and the low tones of "And the Wind Cries Mary" fill the curves of the room.

Everybody smiles. Miranda can feel it. Everyone relaxes out of their annoyance at being stuck at school at night the last day of class before break for a stupid makeup lab. Some of them even start to doze. Miranda coughs and sneezes as loudly as she can. Surely no one suspects that she has given up wiping her face because it will not dry.

The music fades out and there is an audible sigh. "Yeah, well, I could sit here and listen to Hendrix all day, too, folks. But let's get started." He says it mildly, as mildly as he told them how he spent his time at the observatory. The stars rise, and the disembodied voice shows them the Winter Oval, Arcturus, Orion, Gemini. Miranda marks her workbook blindly, the stars, the pages, the electronic arrow swimming. She just has to show that she showed up. That will have to be enough. Now and then she hears something that is not her camouflage cough and sneeze. It is a little squeal, escaping from her, sounding as though it is coming from someone else. I am still covering it, though, she says to herself. No one would recognize that as crying.

The program ends. The lights come up. Miranda, sunglasses back on in a heartbeat, looks intently at the scribbles in her lab workbook. The students file out, dropping the night's exercise torn from their books, perforated edges rough, on the small table next to the door. Miranda sits quietly. No one looks her way. No one sees her. She will sit here until Ramon turns the lights out. There, it is done, except he seems to be finishing something up at the console. Well, she will wait until he leaves, and file out unseen, and drop her torn-out pages off at the department office, through the mail slot in the door.

So she sits, struggling for a composure that she now understands will never come. From beneath the blanket of the darkness she watches Ramon's hands working at the semicircle of the console, which shines under its own light, a warm lamp gentle on the controls as he works them, taking out the program he has just shown. The tape is thick and gigantic, so much bigger than a VHS, and it loads from the top of the funky machine, which looks so ancient although really it is perhaps only ten years old, covered with wires and noisy with its mechanics. There are no buttons, only metal toggles. It is a relic, fit only for the undergraduates in the lab for the humanities majors.

Miranda has never before noticed that there is something wrong with Ramon's hands. Why would she? She has never seen him before or after class except for the time she talked to him about making up the lab, and even then he was still behind the control panel, his hands hidden. She never looks at him during lab, only up at the sky. She has never even watched him enter or leave the planetarium. He is always there when they come in, and he stays after they leave. She has seen only his long hair and mustache and thin face and glasses.

But now, sitting at this sideways angle from him as he works the toggle switches, she can see what is beneath the tiny spot of light. They are not hands so much as claws. Each one is missing fingers, although they are missing different numbers of fingers. Miranda thinks she can count three there on his left hand, two on his right, all of them shorter than normal fingers, more like the digits of animals, and no thumbs. They have not been severed, there are no spaces where anything used to be. He was born that way. The skin looks overly smooth, without the ridges and lines that mark normal hands. This is oddly repulsive-looking to Miranda, far more so than cracked, gnarled, overrough, scarred skin would have been. But she pities him. She pities him from her soul. To go to school with such hands. The taunts of the other children. No wonder he came to the world of the stars for his solace. What are her troubles to his? He must be almost thirty—how has he borne it all this time? Ramon's hands tear right through the already gossamer curtain of separation between Miranda's own troubles and the troubles of the world. Her sobbing renews within her, and though she tries to stifle the sound she cannot, and it comes out as a medium-sized squeal.

Ramon does not appear to hear. He puts another viewing program, another thick cartridge, into the player and cues it up. Then, with a flick of one of his twisted fingers, the light above it is off, and Miranda sits in total darkness.

She hears the dial tone of the speakerphone there at the console, hears it cut off as Ramon picks it up and dials. "Hi, honey." Pause. "Yeah, I'm not sure exactly now, there's some stuff here now I've gotta do." Pause. "Is she in bed? Okay, yeah, please." Pause. "Hi, sweetheart. Yeah, Daddy'll be home after you're asleep. But I'll be home all day tomorrow. You did? You made me a rainbow?" Pause. "That's right, the purple does go on the bottom and not on the top. You're right. That's how the spectrum goes. I'm so proud of you." Pause. "Yes, tomorrow and the day after that and the day after that. And what day is it then? That's right, sweetheart. And we'll be at Grandma's. Okay, noodle. Okay. Good night. I love you, too. Put your mommy back on." Listening. "A few hours, yeah. You know, I think I'm gonna skip the scope time. I know, honey, I'll tell you all about it when

I get there, okay? Okay, babe. Bye." The cut of the click, and soft steps.

And in the darkness, Miranda is all alone.

But then she feels the whisper and even the soft black hair at her ear.

"I don't know what's wrong, but I do know that things get better. Hang in there."

She chokes. It is too much for her. She hid nothing, everyone must have seen, everyone must have heard. What a spectacle. And this is so kind of Ramon, so kind, she feels it in the very depths of her lower belly, as deep in her guts as she can go, this kindness. She tries to smile bravely at him, she feels this is the least she can do in answer to it, but she is too overwhelmed, and the sobs convulse her. No need to be quiet anymore. They are too much for her rib cage, too much for her lungs. Her abdominal muscles are already sore with the constant heaving cries and the suppression of the heaving. She is choking on them. She puts her head down, thinking she will throw up, but she doesn't, only because there is nothing inside her. She heaves dryly, nothing comes out. She sits back up. Her eyes are adjusting to the darkness and she sees that Ramon is flustered, looking about, wondering what to do. Steadying her by her shoulders doesn't help, saying, "Shh, shh," doesn't help, she cannot stop, she cannot stop, she would be wailing if her throat were not so sore, there is only a wheezy screech, but there is power behind the screech, she is letting it out, she is giving it her all, even if her vocal cords are not equal to it. In a kind of desperate rush, Ramon leans in to kiss her.

It is not demanding, this kiss, but neither is it particularly light or gentle. It is a real kiss. Yet there is a fragility to it, as though it is made of glass and will break if Miranda moves. She feels something intangible, like light, a glow, a soft diffusion, traveling from Ramon's mouth to hers. When he takes his mouth away her wails have become simple sobs and hiccups, sheets of tears streaming down her face like a rainstorm, her shoulders shuddering.

"Shh," Ramon says, patting her hand with his and leaning back in his chair. Even in her wretchedness Miranda notices that the skin of that hand feels the same as anyone else's. If you were not looking at it you would never know. A gold wedding band gleams on one of the fingers. "Watch this one," he says. "You'll like this one. Then I'll walk you back to your room."

She feels the swell under her poor exhausted rib cage. "It won't help. I won't be able to sleep." She turns away and feels it begin to start up again. She is so ashamed, so ashamed. "You don't understand. I can't even get up out of this seat. I can't."

"We'll buy some Excedrin PM at Walgreen's on the way back. I'll stay till you fall asleep. I *will* stay."

"How can you?"

"Shh. Watch this one. I like this one."

All around them the midnight sky has been slowly growing lighter, becoming a mystical twilight blue. Now suddenly it is black and shot through with a thousand comets, a rumbling, shooting stars and planets whirling around each other in impossible conjunctions. The recorded voices whisper, from all sides, "What was it? What was it? What could it have been? What was it the shepherds saw? What guided the three kings to the Holy Land?"

The sky empties as suddenly as it was filled and there, on the horizon, it rises. The star, with its single ray that dips far, far below it to the land beneath, to point out the place. Longer and longer the single ray grows, brightening as the star climbs up and up into the heavens, finally resting at the top, at the very center of the sky.

Miranda leans back her head in the chair. Her throat opens, and, for the first time in hours, she breathes.

Witch

When I was a little girl, I used to see witches all the time. I was sure they were witches, not just old women, not just bag ladies hunched over and down on their luck. No, I knew. My twin sister and I agreed on it when, together, we saw them. They were witches, there was no question. Perhaps they were part of a coven? I had read about covens in questionable books, books perhaps not entirely suited to the children's section of the library where I found them, placed there by an unwatchful or sanguine librarian, books about the history of witchcraft, full of painstakingly detailed descriptions of iron maidens, racks, and burnings. Coven or not, there was no reason why there should not be witches in Chicago. Witches inhabit all cities, large and small, all towns, important or inconsequential.

The cold of autumn brought them out the way the heat of summer brings out spiders. Snow came early in my hometown. The blizzards of October gave way to gray slush by Christmas. When we were very tiny, my sister and I walked to Saint Ita's Elementary hand in hand, past the brownstones and the park, the traffic and the skyscrapers and the cathedrals. We cracked the thin ice over the puddles in the alleys, watching the motor oil beneath swirl and glisten in its many iridescent colors, blue and green, rose and gold. The morning the windchill sank to forty below we ducked into a courtyard, a shortcut between Fullerton Parkway and Kemper Place. The yard was all silence, hushed in snow, the small trees covered so thickly with the crystals that they seemed to bear heavy white feathers. The building the courtyard belonged to was rosy stone with faded golden grillwork over its windows and doors. If we could get in the door, we knew, we could cut through the lobby, past the mailboxes and the shadowy dark wooden stairs that led up to the apartments. We could go right through in all that comforting warmth, the feeling returning to our fingers, the iron band of headache around our temples receding, out the back door and then once through that we were almost all the way to school. The snow that was caught in the folds of our scarves would melt, our noses would feel sharp and red, the chill of our sweaty feet inside our snow boots would transform into something prickly and itchy. We would be warm.

We tried the door to the building; it was unlocked. No buzzers in the city in those days, they were still a novelty, so long ago. Inside it was quiet, quiet as the snow. Our boots made their wet prints on the forest-green carpet. We made it past the mailboxes, little mice that we were, and then, just as we came upon the staircase, we saw her. Her. The witch. Padding down the steps utterly without noise as though her feet didn't touch the ground, gripping the grillwork banister. We had trespassed in her lair. Greased lightning, that was how we moved. Now I knew what it meant.

Down the hall and out the back door, I imagine, although we were both too frightened to really remember. But we did not go back the way we came and we found ourselves on Kemper Place across the street from Saint Ita's. So after that, we bore the cold.

But they knew us and followed us, sought us out—or at least, they sought me out. My heart froze icy a year or two later, long after we saw the witch in the rosy building with the courtyard. This time there was one shuffling toward us outside the civic center building in the park where we took ballet. My mother dropped us off but the building was closed because it was a government building and it was election day. The door was locked, but my mother didn't know that. She drove away and we waited for two hours—two hours because we took both classes, beginning and intermediate. We worked very hard and my sister wanted to be a ballet dancer when she grew up. It had been perhaps an hour, we were playing Miss Mary Mack to amuse ourselves, slapping feeling into each other's cold palms as we clapped to the rhyme, Miss Mary Mack, Mack, Mack, all dressed in black, black, black, when the witch crept up the bike path, hobbling in that cold November day. I saw her first, heading toward us, and my whole chest went stock-still, my breath gone. I knew what she was. I could not move or cry out, like in a nightmare. She was different from every other old lady you have ever seen, more bent over, her nose larger, her clothes not just shabby but profoundly drab, gray, and ancient, a scarf over her head like Baba Yaga, the witch who lived in the house that stood on chicken legs and who ate children. We knew her from the fairy tales my father told us.

My sister, afraid but still able to move, nudged me, and with that we could both move, and we ran around the back to where the rest rooms were, hidden by low bare shrubs and bushes, and huddled there against the wall until it was dark. Under cover of the stars we emerged, and the witch was gone, and there was our mother to take us home, and how we ran to her, to the open car door and the warm backseat.

My father was furious with her when he found out what had happened and they had a huge fight about who loved us more. "So you take them!" my mother cried, bitter. He didn't see everything else she had to do, the vacuuming, the lunch packing, the dishwashing. So in the end it was my father who took time off from his grocery store—a small market, called the Golden Apple Grocery, there are none like it anymore—and picked us up from Saint Ita's and took us to ballet. He waited to make sure we got in the door before he drove away.

I tried my own magic as I grew older. My twin sister and I, you see, did not quite fit. I wondered if it was because we saw the witches. No one else seemed to. We were both scrawny and flat-chested, my sister and I, but I was odder. She was second-to-last picked for the team. I was last. I was troubled by warts on my hands; they were continually being burned off with acid at doctor's office visits, so my fingers were always sore. That and my glasses made me afraid of the ball. Or perhaps I would have been afraid of the ball anyway, who's to know?

And so. I bought *Cosmopolitan's Modern Witch's Handbook* from the drugstore shelf, scorched cinnamon sticks with candles in my room with the window open to let the moonlight flow in and make my will be done. I wore the sticks on cords around my neck to maximize the power of the charm—inside my clothes, so no one could see, although they may have noticed in the locker room after gym class.

My sister saw the witches less and less, straining her eyes when I pointed them out, saying, by the time we were thirteen, "I can't believe you remember those games we used to play when we were so little! You should leave the poor bag ladies alone." I did leave them alone, she knew that, I didn't interfere with them. But she had nothing else to say. While my twin sister became more normal, I became more special. For my magic held power I never imagined.

When Sally Carpacio, who had made my sister's and my life unbearable with her catcalls and her laughter, who was always captain of the team, who whooped with her best friend, Jane Champion, when we missed our shots in volleyball, was killed by a car two weeks after eighth-grade graduation, I rejoiced. And, more quietly, unnoticed, so did my sister. "Sally Carpacio is dead!" I cried when we heard at church, and there was glee in my voice, and my sister looked at me, eyes wide, then looked pointedly at where she knew the cinnamon sticks hung beneath my white blouse. She smiled calmly—a saintly smile, a beatific smile. "Wow," she whispered.

My mother was horrified. "That poor girl—who would have thought?" she said when we came home that Sunday. She didn't know I had burned the black incense in my room, pricked my finger to get the blood, said the proper incantations, despite all the warnings in my witchcraft books, the cautions in *Cosmopolitan's Modern Witch's Handbook* about working something so irreversible as a death spell, about the things you invite in when you do such a thing. I was young. Even I, unhappy and strange and little and odd as I was, lived in a world of no consequences, like all the young. My mother didn't know what it was like, no one to sit with at lunch, looking at Jane Champion with her long blond hair, so beautiful, wanting to be her, and Jane catching me, making a face at me and calling me a weirdo. Better revenge to kill her friend than her. Better to leave her all alone. My mother might have been thinking of us more, me and my sister, than that nasty, mean-spirited girl. Where was her kindness, her concern for *us*? My sister looked in my eyes, her own the same color, the same shape, the same flame behind them, those eyes locking with mine. Whatever she laughed or trilled away, she knew. She remembered the witches.

I had done my work. It was enough. All things were in my power. It would never let me down.

Whatever I asked for, the high priestess of the witches, the all-powerful goddess, gave me, which was more than any god or virgin at Saint Ita's, who somehow never saw or remedied Sally's and Jane's many small cruelties, had ever done. I achieved. I was still odd and apart, but I got what I wanted. Perfect grades. The right university, the very best one, a whole year early. Prizes, honors. I was not so scrawny anymore. The internship fell into my wart-ravaged hands. I did well at it, was offered a job with all the money I could want, especially all a strange little young woman like me could want, who did not buy fancy clothes or fabulous boots and wanted only gloves for her hands and a store of candles and incense and expensive herbs from the occult bookstore. I was sharp. I was, in a way, charmed.

I was awarded every promotion—or awarded them to myself—and where I found enemies, they disappeared. My sister stayed closer to home for college and left it after two years, marrying a warm and generous man, a wholesale dealer in upscale seafood, salmon and swordfish and tuna and oysters. They moved to the Northwest together and had beautiful children. She had forgotten her own wish to be special, to be a ballerina, a sugar plum fairy exquisite upon the stage. I would have given it to her had she asked, but she never did, and she had not the magic herself, it seemed. And her husband had no need of a magical wife.

I met *him*, then, at the height of all my powers. My first glimmer of light in a grim, unpopular life. I was so used to men who never quite wanted to name me as their girlfriend, did elaborate dances around never calling quite enough, so that I would not get mistaken ideas, would not get my beaten-down hopes up. But he loved me. He did not even know about the magic, and he treasured me. He held me tenderly. He kissed my hands and knew how they must have tortured me. He was scrawny, like I had been. He had missed all the shots at volleyball, too. He understood. We knew each other so well already, before we met. And I had not even had to work a spell to bring him. I loved him.

He wanted to be famous.

He did not know what he wanted to be famous at. Perhaps at words, he was good with words, he had learned to be since he was not good with baseballs or footballs. Or with knowledge—he had studied, like I had, while waiting to be picked last for the team. Or music. He liked music and his voice was clear and pure. Or perhaps the stage, he was excellent at pretending to the world that he was other than what he was. He did not know which of these things, or any other, should be bringing him his ambition. He only knew that, in fact, he should already *have been* famous, that he was too old already. Young as he was, he did not feel young, and fame years ago would not have been too early. He was as hollow inside as I was.

I so wanted for him to be famous.

He never asked me to do anything. At first, of course, he did not even know what I could do. I scorched my cinnamon sticks. Nothing. I burned the green and gold candles with a hair from his head. Nothing. Made a wax doll, saying the proper incantations. Nothing.

I was not then like the hardened city witches my sister and I used to see. There was too much proximity to other people in the city. I was too close to the distracting swirling energies of the human race. I could not focus on just one man, even this one I loved. Working strong magic was like spotting comets or watching meteor showers, best done away from city lights. And this was the strongest magic I had ever tried to work. But to be famous, he needed to be with the teeming masses, in the thickest part of the stream. We compromised. He agreed to a place within easy train distance of downtown. Then, a year later, at my insistence, we went farther away, to a place an hour's drive away, a place where we could still hear the crickets at night, where old-fashioned Halloween ghosts made of sheets hung from the trees and followed trick-or-treating children, where apple and pumpkin stands still stood by the roadside, where the chimneys smoked at Christmas. A place where the ravens flew over our house and our heads. Ravens circled above me when I walked out. Beneath a cloud of them, I sacrificed a nightingale in the quiet, my first real blood sacrifice, and begged its spirit, with its clear voice that caught the ears of all, that commanded attention and cried out "Look at me!" to inhabit him. But the farther away from humankind we went, the less well known he became, until finally almost no one knew him at all but me.

He wanted it so very much. The adulation of the world was the only thing that could make him feel whole. But still the goddess of the witches did not answer him.

I read and reread all my books. I bought better ones. *The Spiral Dance, Magick and the Faerie Tradition,* the works of Z Budapest. I read that magic was about changing one's own consciousness, so of course it was very difficult to do for someone else. Results cannot be guaranteed. Particularly if one does not have permission from the object of one's magic. I screwed up my courage, confessed this odd practice of mine to the one man who had ever loved me. I told him that I wanted him to be rich and famous and chosen and special if that was the only thing besides my love that he needed to be happy, that I wanted him to win the great lottery of life. I most humbly asked him to let me do my spells in his name and with his knowledge. He laughed, which was infrequent, but said, "Okay, go ahead. Go to town. Knock yourself out. Do your magic for me."

I could see he did not quite understand its power. What might he have said if he knew my magic could bring money and glittering prizes or kill a young girl, as I chose?

I cast my circles in the field, naked in the cold at dawn, invoked the four directions, banished with bells and cries and a sacred broom the evil spirits who stood in his way. The ravens still followed me, floating only a little way above my head. I burned incense of success and abundance. That was as close as I could get, success and abundance. There is no incense prescribed for fame. It is a dangerous thing to play with, more dangerous even than death. I did not know that then. I did not know that fame is as hollow as he was, as I was. I told the universe that I would give whatever was required that was mine. But he remained unknown, unseen by the world. I would come across him, his face in his long fine hands. "What's the matter?" I would ask. "You know," he would answer.

He would need to join me. That was it. And we would need to go far away even from where we were, closer to the source.

We went to Europe, to a cave outside Prague, the birthplace of the Celts before their migration, the place of the witches, the wicca, they who bend the world to their will. Here was where they began the ancient worship, the making of the gods and goddesses from the elemental forces. The magic. As we made our way in the feral cats clustered around me, mewing, and ate from my hand, and I was at home. From this place, I thought, it will begin. He will be famous.

We did our magic in the cave, dressed in bear skins around the fire at night on All Hallow's Eve, when the veil between the worlds is at its thinnest. It was a long dance. It made my joints ache and my back bend, so I had to walk stooped over afterward and I do to this day. My bones have never recovered from the dance. But it was a fair price, if my love would be granted what he wanted. I tried to scry into the flame of the fire, to see the future, to divine what was to come, but I saw nothing.

Nothing. The spell did not work.

I had to leave. I could not watch him not be famous anymore, I could not watch my magic fail anymore. I could not see his misery. I had failed. I had to turn my back. I could not help him win the great lottery. Fortune would not turn toward him, the priestess of the witches was mute for him, for him and me. I could not bear it. Perhaps if I were to give him up, she would relent. Or perhaps, from afar, I could do him more good. Horrible, to think of him all alone.

"Don't go!" he cried. But I heard it as from the other end of a long tunnel, fading away, his hands upheld, beseeching, in surrender.

I wrote to my sister. She had gone far from the city lights herself, living with her husband in a village by the water where her own daughters played, plunging into the sea without a care. She wrote me back, inviting me to come and stay. Perhaps, I thought, I could begin again there, do a little mild magic to begin with, perhaps even regain my power, drawing strength from the company of my sister.

She gasped when she saw my face. I did not realize how much it had changed, nor how bent my back had become. I did little charms around the house, halfheartedly, with candles, trying to begin gently. But I think I frightened my sister's children with my mutterings and coarsened skin and anyway it was not enough to be in that charming, wild place by the sea. I was not alone enough with my failed workings. I needed more. I bought a little house, far out of the village, with no running water. I see my sister rarely now, and I will not bring her to my tiny hut in the woods.

I do not think of him often anymore, except to know he is not famous—even in these woods, I know I would know if he were, I would dream of it—and so he is unhappy and alone. When I do think of him I weep and howl at the orange moon, the harvest moon in the black sky. The wind turns colder, smells of char, and the leaves are crisp as paper under my feet. The cold is coming on its muffled, pale paws. The winter approaches.

Today in the early morning that is white with mist and fog I stand on the ridge above the village and watch the chimneys smoke, and I know my place. I know where I belong. Back, I must retrace my steps, while the ravens follow and still twist and turn above me. Back through the village, through the countryside, back to the city where I grew up, the city of my birth, the city where the hobbling ladies first found me and marked me. I will befriend the pigeon, the bat, the mouse, the rat. I will wander the streets and parks among all the teeming masses who do not and would not see me. I will not hear their buzzing anymore, it will not distract me now, I am far above it, hearing only the movement of the curling clouds. In the cold I will make my way through the hushed courtyard, silent with snow, and up the stairs, to the room that has been readied for me. There, perhaps, with great focus, great discipline, I may recover my powers. I have all the time in the world, though I will not be in time for *him*. I will outlive him, I will outlive all of them, my sister and her husband, their children. Death will not come for *me*. I will pad through the hallways, up and down the banisters, across the bicycle paths, forever.

Men Have More
Upper-Body Strength

In the green twilight of the green day, in Sheila O'Rourke's big, trashy, glittery house on the seedy side of town, which was covered with fluttery green paper decorations from Walgreen's, among all that green, Brigid sat at Sheila's kitchen table. She cut shamrocks from green construction paper, taping them up on the refrigerator and walls, watching Sheila cook green rice and green tamales, getting ready for the party for Saint Patrick's Day. Sheila had hung green crepe-paper snakes in great webs from the ceiling in the living room. "He drove the snakes out of Ireland, the fucker," she said, "but there *were* no snakes in Ireland, they mean the pagans when they say that, snakes were symbols of the goddess, it's in the prayer of Saint Patrick, Saint Patrick's Breastplate. 'Protect me from the enchantments of women or smiths or druids.'" But Sheila liked a good excuse for partying as well as anybody else.

So Brigid cut the shamrocks from the green paper and marked them with green glitter glue, and they talked, and Sheila said, around the time that she was cutting up the green pepper to go in the green rice, "I make Boniface Tyler nervous."

"Why?" asked Brigid. She had a crush on Boniface Tyler and liked the relief of hearing him talked about, of saying his name. She had not had a crush in some time and so was protective of this one, telling no one, not even Sheila. She was sure she had not yet given it away. She would have liked the edge of knowing how to make Boniface Tyler nervous.

Sheila put her mouth down close to Brigid's ear, although they were alone, and looked around the kitchen as though someone might be listening, hiding among the leprechauns on the paper tablecloth or behind the keg of green beer. Outside, beyond the window, they could already hear the roars and the calls of the drinkers in the sports bars and dives on the corners. Sheila began by whispering but ended in a triumphant cackle. "I raped him!" she cried, and whooped and danced a few steps around the room.

Brigid looked at her friend. Sheila was already in her party dress, which was twenty years older than she was, ratty emerald-green crinkly satin with a green crinoline, trimmed with black velvet piping. Her black stockings were so destroyed they looked like spiderwebs, and her feet shone in cracked patent-leather dark green and silver buckled shoes, very high-heeled, sprinkled with sequins. Sheila was not pretty—she was too bony on the top, too wide on the bottom, her features too blunt with no fineness to them, her nose thick, no cheekbones to speak of. Her skin was rough with mild acne scars, her hair rough, too, from all the colors she had dyed it, dark auburn tonight and braided into a hundred long coils, each tied at the end with a ribbon. It amazed Brigid, who was herself quite diminutive and beautiful, Black Irish with her shining jet-black hair and glowing blue-green eyes and fine skin, that men had once paid money to see Sheila with her clothes off. Sheila had been a stripper in Japan, had tripped on old-fashioned blotter-paper acid in Mexico, had hitchhiked through Germany with two brothers, Nigerian brothers, and she had had no qualms about doing them both in turn as they toured the provinces. She had lived in a dozen cities in neighborhoods it would never have occurred to Brigid to go into. Brigid liked, she knew, to go slumming in Sheila's life, of which she was not particularly proud. But that did not stop her asking for tales of Sheila's adventures.

"You what?" Brigid said. "I don't get it."

Sheila repeated it, again softly and close to Brigid's ear. "I. Raped. Him."

"I don't get it. I don't understand. He's a guy. How could you *rape* him? How could you do that?"

"It was easy."

"*How?*"

Sheila looked at Brigid with a tilt of her head, frustrated, as though she should have known. She smiled, as though to a child.

"You know when someone's trying to fuck you and he's wriggled between your legs but you don't want to, so you kind of straighten your legs, put your knees down? You know, so he hasn't got the access and he can't quite get it?"

"Well . . ." Brigid answered. She had not been in that particular situation, but yes, she thought she saw what Sheila meant.

"I just put my knees up!" Sheila cried gleefully. "I mean he was right there and he was already hard, so I just wrapped my legs around him and wriggled around a little and, you know, he just slipped in, there was nowhere else for his dick to go." She twirled around, swirling her twisted hair in a full circle, the glitter-green ribbons at the ends of the braids sparkling in the uneven light of the kitchen, then stopped, her head again tilted to one side. "Kind of a date rape." She shrugged, opened a silverware drawer, and rummaged in it until she found a film canister. She held it up.

"Yeah, sure," said Brigid. There was half a joint left. Sheila lit it, inhaled, and passed it to Brigid.

"This is what happened," she said. "I went with Tommy Boy the last time he went on tour to Seattle because I wasn't doing anything and he said, well, hang with me and do a go-go dancing thing with the band. You know Tommy, right, he plays electric fiddle, sometimes I cut his hair?"

Brigid nodded. Sheila had been to beauty school and now she cut hair and did makeup at a cheap and highly successful salon decorated on all the walls with broken glass. That was how Brigid had met her. Sheila had cut Brigid's hair in soft, uneven wisps, got it to look wavy for the first time, a feathery dark halo around her ivory skin and clear red-tinged cheeks. She had looked like an angel, had never been so beautiful.

"So Boniface was in Portland for some reason, I forget why, and he came up to Seattle to meet us." She stopped, like that explained everything.

"But . . ." Brigid was persistent. "Was it really rape? Did you ask him? Did he say no?"

"Oh, he said no all right."

"But . . ." still she groped. "Why?"

"Oh, he does this really sick thing, Brigid. Whenever he's away from home, he's in a club, he's at a party, you *know* how he is, he's cute, a lot of girls just fall over him. . . ."

"Not you."

"No." She smiled, inhaled again as Brigid passed her the dope. "Not me." She sucked, passed it back, became animated. "So they look at him like he's some Calvin Klein ad or some shit, and they get this *expression* on their faces." She mimed it—wrinkled forehead, eyebrows gathered up and toward the middle, trembling chin, a kittenlike mewing sound. "Makes me *sick*." The joint was out as it came to her again. She lit it in the gas flame of the stove, her coarse braids falling close to the burner.

"Jesus, Sheila, watch it."

"Sorry. So anyway. Boniface Tyler will do anything but. *Anything.* He'll really get into it, he'll have all his clothes off, he'll have his dick in your mouth, you'll be having a good time, thinking, Yeah, boy, you want to do this, let's do it—and then he just nixes the whole thing. He'll say, 'I have a girlfriend. I can't go all the way. I'm sorry.' Go all the way, he actually *says* that."

"Does he? Have a girlfriend?" asked Brigid, whose heart had quickened and then sunk when she heard the words.

"Oh, yeah. Amanda or something."

Brigid knew her. Slim, blond. She had talked to her once, at a show.

"But he thinks it's all okay as long as he doesn't actually fuck someone?"

"Men," said Sheila. "Assholes."

Brigid was silent.

Sheila went on. "It's this really sick ego thing, that's all it is. He just needs to do this to women. I'm just bold, Brigid," she said, answering Brigid's look. "*You* should be bold. I get to fuck all the boys I want to fuck, and it's just because I'm bold. I just ask. I'm shameless. Be bold. They hardly ever say no. When they do . . ." She smiled charmingly, pleased with herself, and shrugged, palms up, like she couldn't help what she did.

"Wow," said Brigid. She wondered something but it took her a minute to ask. "Was he any good?"

"He came like that," Sheila said, snapping her fingers. "Maybe it had been a while."

Brigid put her head down. Her scalp tingled and she didn't like it. The leprechauns on the tablecloth leered at her. "Fuck, Sheila, I've got head rushes. Fuck, fuck, fuck."

"Here, you should eat something," Sheila said, spooning some of the green stew bubbling on the stove into a bowl. But Brigid looked at it and her stomach turned over. She shook her head.

"You can't be pregnant, can you?" Sheila asked. She grinned like one of the leering leprechauns.

Brigid smiled, shook her head again. This last was meant ironically. They both knew the idiocy of trying to be funny by asking nauseated women if they were pregnant. People had no idea what they were fucking saying.

Brigid knew exactly how long her own pregnancy had lasted. Seven weeks. They wouldn't take it out until it had been seven weeks. She wanted them to do it when she first found out, at five weeks, but they said they couldn't. They had to wait until seven, it wasn't safe otherwise, it was the law. Nowhere, not even in *Our Bodies, Ourselves,* had Brigid ever before or since heard any mention of the convulsing cramps that ruthlessly twisted the side of her abdomen where the embryo was implanted. On her it was the left. The nurse practitioner said yes, that cramping can be very painful, it's caused by the uterus expanding—God, thought Brigid with horror, can't they do anything to stop that?—and there's nothing for it but aspirin. Which didn't help.

"I hate this thing," she had told Sheila over the phone.

"I know," said Sheila. "I hated it, too. It had no right to be inside of me. I was so fucking mad. You could try pennyroyal tea."

"They specially told me not to get any ideas about that. They said it wasn't safe."

"Fuckers."

They told her at the clinic that her body would be exactly the same as it was before, nothing different, nothing changed, but Brigid thought they had lied. She thought she got carsick a lot easier than before.

"Put your head down," Sheila commanded now. After a few minutes she said, "Better?"

"Yeah."

"Want me to do your makeup?"

The big, soft makeup brushes—only the best, Sheila bought only the best, most expensive ones—stroking Brigid's face, yes, that was what she needed.

Sheila's room was a vast bright carnival of color, of shiny old clothes, red thongs and yellow and orange bathrobes and sapphire stockings strewn everywhere, floral sheets and crazy mismatched furniture covered in beads, a hula girl clock, Marvin the Martian dolls. Sheila's makeup case, the size of a large airplane carry-on bag, was the same, colors both vivid and pale, wine red, soft pink, electric blue, and neon green exploding out of it. But Sheila knew its order. And though chaotic, the brushes and powders and creams were set in meticulously clean compartments, shimmering spotless. This was, after all, how Sheila earned her living.

They were quiet while Sheila worked, except for saying now and then that they wished it would snow. They looked out the window at the slush raining out of the hard charcoal sky—not so unusual, really, for a Saint Patrick's Day sky in their part of the world, where spring had usually not gelled by March seventeenth and the winter had three or four limping, stale weeks left in it. It hardly meant spring, despite all the green. The earth still looked barren, the trees lifeless. "If it would snow," Sheila said, "the world would be prettier then, all pearly white. Not dirty gray. Not like it is now."

Brigid stared at her face in the mirror while Sheila opened the drawers of her kit. A movie played in her head, a movie of Boniface Tyler on top of Sheila, him saying, "No," while she just wrapped her legs around him and started pushing. Sheila's cats, green bows on their necks, crept soundlessly about, sat silky in Brigid's lap, and moved on. Brigid and Sheila heard, carried on the swirling air of the darkening sky, behind the slush, the far-off howls and roars of the partyers at the watering holes. Brigid visualized those places, decked out for the holiday, shamrock coasters with logos under every beer, Budweiser, Guinness. The alcohol would already be so far past flowing, it had flowed and flowed and then some, and it would flow more yet. *Erin Go Bragh*—Ireland forever. Kiss me, I'm Irish. Honorary leprechaun.

"Raping a guy," Brigid said. "I mean, Jesus."

"It wasn't that big a deal," Sheila answered absently. She searched for the right shades.

"Did you ever take one of those self-defense courses? The ones where they teach you to have an aggressive attitude? You know, and you beat up the guys in the padded suits? And they teach you to fight even if you're already on the ground?"

Sheila shook her head. "But I saw something about it on TV. There's all kinds of things you can do. Like, you shouldn't try to punch and fight with your hands because you'll lose. Men have more upper-body strength. That's why no matter how hard you try, you'll always throw like a girl. Men can throw straight from the shoulder—they've got all that mass. Women have stronger legs, lower-body strength. Lower center of gravity."

"So what are you supposed to do?"

"Kick. Men don't usually kick when they fight, so they don't expect it."

"It's still not fair," she said.

"Hmm?" Sheila smoothed powder on Brigid's face.

"I want to be able to throw like a guy. I want upper-body strength."

"I know." She hummed a little ditty while she worked. " 'And Paddy dear and did you hear the news that's goin' round, the shamrock is forbid by law to grow on Irish ground. Saint Patrick's Day no more we'll keep, his color can't be seen, for there's a bloody law agin' the wearin' of the green.' "

The shadow she chose was the color of fir trees and Brigid's eyes glowed like the blue flames of a gas jet beneath it. Green sparkle mascara she fished out, for Brigid's lashes. She made her lips a ruby, ruby red.

" 'Oh the wearin' of the green, oh the wearin' of the green, they're hanging men and women for the wearin' of the green . . .' "

*   *   *

When they came downstairs again the marijuana had worn off and they were only pleasantly tired, ready to be woken up by friends and drink. The band was there to set up, Tommy Boy with his fiddle, his green derby a concession to the night, and his friends with their drum kit and amps. They put themselves in front of Sheila's window at the far end of the living room, surrounded by cardboard leprechauns hung on the walls. Brigid hoped the music would be loud.

A half hour later, beneath the green paper pythons floating from the ceiling, Tommy struck up a kind of Celtic rockabilly. People were walking around now with their drinks, the room not yet full but lively, clearly with more to come. No one rang the doorbell after Tommy—Sheila left everything open and guests all let themselves in, a flow of people dressed in green and black under the parkas and ski masks they wore because of the cold.

The kegs were out and flowing, the refrigerator full from the top to bottom shelf with amber bottles. No one touched the buffet of green food, but they would get hungry, Sheila said, just wait and see. She loosened the end of one of her green crepe-paper snakes and swung it at her guests. They ducked and went on talking.

"Rub my neck, will you, doll? I'm tense," Sheila said. Brigid was excellent at back rubs. She carried some memory of everything that had ever felt good on her and could apply it. People looked at her hands with undisguised longing as Sheila moaned her pleasure.

"Hey, Sheila," Brigid whispered. "What's he doing here?" There, through the thick cloud of cigarette smoke over Sheila's shoulders, was Boniface Tyler in his green short-sleeved dress shirt. She saw him first eyeing Sheila, then eyeing her, and she thought she saw suspicion in the looks but couldn't be sure, and she wondered if Sheila had been telling the truth, or embroidering her date-rape adventure for Brigid's benefit.

Sheila glanced at him, unconcerned. "Probably couldn't think of a good excuse not to come," she said. "Probably easier just to show up for a while. This *is*"—she turned and smiled—"the social event of the season." She turned to a friend of hers, a young red-headed boy Brigid didn't know, and danced away with him. Brigid lost sight of them when Tommy put down his fiddle between songs, but then she turned and found herself blocked by Boniface's shoulder. He was tall. He smelled good. Fuck, he's gorgeous, she thought.

He took a sip of his beer and motioned to her hands, so recently kneading Sheila's shoulders. "You good at that?" he asked.

"Oh, yeah."

"Give me one? Okay?" he said.

"Sure."

And though Brigid could only see the back of his golden-brown head, she could tell he had spotted Sheila again, by the front door, and was watching her, perhaps warily. Sheila turned to smile brightly at the two of them before she let herself be led out onto the front porch by the redhead. Brigid actually felt Boniface's muscles relax, give up a little of their resistance to her fingers.

When she touched him she could again see him and Sheila together on a bed. In her vision, Sheila wore fuchsia and black lace.

"Jesus," he said. "She is a crazy one, huh?" He turned around to face Brigid.

"Why?" she asked.

"Thanks for the back rub," he said, and he walked into the kitchen for more beer.

Well, shit, said Brigid to herself.

Alone now, she headed for the porch. In the cold and dark of the front yard more of Sheila's guests were milling around, and Sheila was clearing a place on the ice that covered the driveway. Wood and twigs were stacked against the side of the house, and she and her redheaded friend started to pile them on the cleared circle.

Behind her, Brigid heard the sound of retching. Someone she didn't know was throwing up green. She held his head, her face turned away, and called to Sheila, "What are you doing?"

"A bonfire!" Sheila cried back gleefully, and the redheaded boy smiled ruefully. "St Patrick liked bonfires! He used to have them at Easter, to win over the pagans, to celebrate spring coming." Sheila scratched a fireplace match against one of the roughest pieces and tossed it into the pile, and the newspaper beneath the kindling shot flames up into the sky.

"Thanks," whoever had been retching muttered to Brigid. "Sorry." He went back inside. Brigid watched the flames die a little, then catch the kindling, then the heavy wood. The band started up, she could hear them through the windows, and, chilled, she turned back toward the door. Sheila stayed a while longer, the fire dancing in her eyes, the light catching off the emerald sequins and the silver buckles of her shoes. Tommy Boy was singing, another man's song but a good one nevertheless—"I feel so good I'm gonna break somebody's heart tonight."

Brigid danced her way to the Irish whiskey on the buffet table. Sheila was right, they had gotten hungry, the dishes were almost empty. But there was a clean plastic shot glass. She poured, downed one shot, downed two.

* * *

When Boniface Tyler had gotten drunker, coming up on three A.M., Brigid ran into him again by the fridge. The kegs were empty, and though the crowd was thinning some, there were plenty of people still downing the bottles that were left. He saw her, opened the refrigerator, and, gallant but sloppy, took out two beers and offered her one.

"No, thanks," she said. "I already had a couple and I'm a light-weight." She hesitated, thought, said, "I've always been really irritated that men were bigger than me and could drink more."

He smiled at her. He really seemed to see her now, despite the alcohol. And he wasn't that out of it, not really. God, she thought, Sheila is right, this is easy. It's like I woke something up, reminding him that I'm smaller than him and he's bigger than me. And it turns him on.

She looked straight back at him and held his gaze for longer than she needed to.

"Is your girlfriend here?" she asked. "She's so nice. I had a talk with her once, at one of Tommy Boy's shows. What's her name? Amanda?"

"Miranda," he said. "She's not here."

"Oh."

"Actually, she didn't want to come."

"Oh."

"Things aren't going so great."

He kneaded his own neck on one side. "My shoulders are still really stiff." He had extra confidence, extra smugness now. Well, Brigid knew that attitude in men, when they were just buzzed enough. She liked men when they were like that—easy, playful, liking to be caught in small subterfuges.

"Oh, I'll do it again. But let's go upstairs, so everybody else won't want one."

He nodded. Brigid thought, What the fuck. What the fuck.

He lay on Sheila's crazy flowered sheets, there among all the colors, and murmured, "That's great, oh man, that's great," while she kneaded his shoulders. He sat up suddenly and took off his green shirt, showing the white knit T underneath. He lay back down again without a word. Brigid went on. Her thumbs and the joints of her fingers ached. But she loved the way his back felt. That was one of her favorite things, the way male backs felt under worn-thin cotton T-shirts. They were always smoother than she expected, sometimes even as smooth as her own skin. She wanted to put her cheek down on his shoulder and breathe deeply but she felt like it wasn't time yet. Instead she said, "I read palms, too."

"No kidding," he said, immediately turning over and sitting up. "Where'd you learn?"

"My mom taught me," she said. "She's kind of a . . ." What was her mother? Brigid saw her with all the other mothers, around the kitchen table with the TV on in the afternoon, coffee and soda bread and tea and the leaves. Just for fun, said her mother. So they all said. But they knew how, just the same.

He held out his hand.

"I need both of them," she said. "Relax them." She cradled the hands, struck and faintly pleased by how big and callused they were compared with her own, and saw the chained health line and the nick of a scar across the right life line.

"Are you right-handed?" she asked.

"Uh-huh."

"Well, you have a lot of health problems. You always have." She looked up and he nodded, staring at his palms. "And there's one really major issue in your life, one big problem you feel you can't get the better of, but it's something you cause yourself." She turned his hand to look at the lines at the side of his little finger. There was just one that was well marked. "One big love of your life," she said. She looked up at his face. Such pretty eyes, she thought. Even the intense, unflappable gold of his eyes shaded toward green tonight. "That's it," she said. "I don't remember how to do any more." They smiled at each other.

He put his hands on her and his fingertips were tight and hard on her arms just below the shoulders as he leaned in to kiss her. She wondered idly if he would leave fingertip bruises and kind of hoped he would. Proof of how much he wanted her, how hard it was for him to keep his hands off her.

He's good at kissing, she thought as his tongue passed into her mouth, and after a minute she added in her head, in an anger that she didn't understand, he's good at kissing, the mother-fucker, the shit.

His mouth was soft, his tongue was soft, he didn't ram it in and start pushing it down her throat or let it loll around all over inside her mouth. It was all slow and easy for him. He kissed down her neck, kissed her breasts, stuck his hands under her dress. She wanted so much to touch his shoulders, so she put her hands on them and that was where she felt him, a kind of quick jumpiness in his narrow muscles, like something she sometimes noticed within herself, a kind of restlessness caged by bone and skin, although with her it was more in her legs. That was where the center of him was, in his sharp, coltish shoulders, right there where her hands were. His back was calmer and the sensation of something underneath his skin tapered off when her fingertips grazed the smooth vertical curve down his shoulder blade toward his waist. But still it felt great, it felt terrific, his back was alive and moving like a wave, warm and smooth like he had spent the day in the sun. She lay back and he stretched out on top of her and she could feel him getting hard against her. She pressed her mouth against his furiously and ran her fingers under the waistband of his jeans.

He finished kissing her and moved so that he was lying beside her with one of his hands in her hair. "This is nice," he said. He smiled sleepily. Brigid stroked his belly under his shirt and, as she kissed him again, she unzipped his jeans and moved them, along with his boxers, over his hips. He took her hands in his and kissed them.

"Mmm," he said, and put her hands on the back of his neck and wrapped his arms around her. She took one hand away and used it to help her wriggle out of her panties and slip them over her ankles. Then she pressed her body against his as hard as she could.

He laughed. "Mmm, cut it out, I'll do something really foolish," he said, smiling.

Be bold, Brigid thought.

"I want to do something foolish," she said, smiling back.

"No, look," he said, holding her an arm's length away. "I'm sorry. I guess . . . I mean, I know I didn't say it very well. I'm really, really sorry, but I'm still with my girlfriend. I think that's not going to be going on for much longer. I mean it. I've seen you before—I like you, I'm, you know, I'm attracted to you. Maybe we could see each other again. It's just, while I'm still with her, I don't want to cheat on her. You know? You understand?"

"You don't want to cheat on her?" Brigid was still smiling. "You're not cheating on her now?"

His face reddened, which looked unpleasantly florid against all of his gold and green, and made her almost not want him for a second. It passed. After a pause he said, "Well, no, not really."

"That's silly," she said.

He answered, "I don't know what else to say."

She turned away from him. For a few seconds, on this night of green, this night of the color of spring and new places and new lives, she wanted to start fresh, she did want to see him again, see if they liked each other, see if he wanted to be her boyfriend. And then she didn't, and she thought he was probably lying. Then she wanted to again. Then she didn't. When she didn't, she was angry, and in her anger she looked at him, still with his pants half off and his T-shirt pulled up, and said, "What's the matter? Don't you want to?"

"Well, yeah, I want to, it's not that. . . . Jesus Christ, I didn't think you'd be mad." He laughed shortly, self-consciously. "I'm trying to be an okay guy here."

Okay, she thought. Stay calm. Don't get desperate, don't go

all off balance. That's what he wants, she surprised herself by thinking. She knew she was pissed off, but knowing it didn't seem to help. She needed to do this, she just needed to, even though she knew that if she could get back to where she was before, before he had pulled her hands away from him, she would see that she shouldn't.

"Okay," she said coldly.

"Well, look," he said. He stroked her back from where he lay, still trying to be friends. "Maybe we should just go downstairs."

She sighed. "Yeah." Duplicitous, she thought. I am being duplicitous. I know exactly what I am about to do. She said to him, "Listen, this all feels weird now. Let's not leave it quite like this, okay? Kiss me again, just for a minute? And then we can go back to the party? What do you think?"

He smiled. He looked pleased. "Okay," he whispered. He inclined his head with its warm half-open mouth up toward her and stretched out his arms to hold her while his eyelids drifted shut. When her face twisted toward him she slipped on top of his body, grabbed his wrists to pull his arms down to his sides, and rested her knees squarely on the insides of his elbows. She kept her eyes and the set of her brows playful. Men have more upper-body strength, she thought. Women have stronger legs and better balance.

"Hey, ouch," he said, but he laughed, and still he kissed her as she bent over him, a wide, open, long kiss that fed on her mouth because it was the last one. And he liked it. She could tell. While he kissed her, Brigid reached down between them to the top of his slim thigh and rested her hand there for a minute, hesitating, and she thought he made a sound and she moved her hand and she could feel he could still do it, he was still hard. He was motionless for a second, tense and waiting, and then he broke away from her mouth and said, laughing again, "Hey, cut it out." He tried to reach down and pull her hand away but she wouldn't let him. They were both smiling and giggling, as though this were a joke and she would give it up any minute now. With her hands she pushed his wrists down into the mattress and she was very stable as she knelt over him, very hard to throw off balance, though he twisted underneath her. With one foot she directed a quick, cutting kick inward toward his leg with the sharp heel of her shoe, unsure of what she'd get, and she thought she got the tender spot just at the edge of his shin, and his mouth opened in surprise and she just pushed herself onto him until he was inside of her, and she grabbed him hard by his soft hair so that his eyes filled with tears, and he jerked upward, arching his back, although whether in an involuntary betrayal of pleasure or an effort to get her off of him she didn't know, and anyway it only had the effect of forcing him deeper inside of her. He grabbed her waist and tried to push her away but she dug with her knees and toes into the soft mattress and bore down on him with all her weight.

"What are you doing, for Chrissake, what the hell do you think you're doing?" he spat out, not loudly, more like he was hissing the words. What was he going to do, call for help? Really, *call for help?* And there was something going on with him, too, she thought with satisfaction, as though now that it had started, it wasn't easy for him to stop. He was hard inside of her, after all. Wow, she thought, could I say he was asking for it? Could I say that deep down he wanted it?

She considered punching him in the mouth but then she decided not to because it might upset her balance and the strength of her hold on him, and she was just starting to find the right rhythm to move and still keep him pinned down, and she didn't want to get into punching because he would win at that because he'd be better at it. But she dug her nails into the flesh of his wrists. His face started to flush and twist and his teeth to clench and unclench against little sounds that kept escaping from deep in his chest, and it seemed that he was struggling to keep quiet, as though he had decided that if she was going to continue this, then by God at least he wasn't going to make any noise. Brigid stopped being able to look at his eyes.

But this is easy, she thought defiantly. My God, this is easy! I could have been doing this all along. He was mouthing "Jesus." His body seemed to relax a little but she thought it was a trick. She felt nothing that reminded her of arousal. She wasn't going to come and she knew it. She wasn't even turned on. She didn't care. That had nothing to do with anything.

She saw something cross his face, a sort of pulling of his mouth into a tight line before it relaxed, and before she could stop herself she thought, Does he think I'm ugly? Is my ass too wide? Are my breasts too small? Then she was disappointed in herself. "I don't care what you think of me," she muttered, moving on top of him. "I don't care." Watching his face, she thought, that was what counted. Nothing mattered, nothing, except what she was doing to him.

And it hurt, she was doing it so hard. And she thought he knew that, she thought he could feel it, and was doing his best to keep it that way. Fuck you, she thought. Fuck you, do you think I can't take getting fucked a little too hard? You have no idea what I can take.

He came like *that*, scowling and biting his lip. Maybe it had been a while.

She planned to stay on him until his eyes opened. But it took a long time. She looked down at his eyelids twitching with the movement underneath them. She waited to hear the familiar sound of a man's breath slowing, but his face stayed red and his panting didn't stop. She knew he might call her "bitch" and hiss "fuck you" and she steeled herself for that, but he lay still. Finally she eased off of him and reached up to his shoulder to shake it.

He didn't shrug her hand off. He was immobile, like metal, like lead. She rolled over and stretched out next to him on the bed, pulled her skirt down. He turned his back to her momentarily, and then he stood up. He did it slowly, resting on the edge of the bed with his fingers spread out flat next to his thighs, supporting himself even while he was still sitting, using his hands as leverage to get to his feet, sighing as he rose as if he were old. He got himself zipped and buttoned and Brigid watched him test his legs on his first step or two, like a tired horse, before he crossed the room to Sheila's vanity and picked up one of her sleek makeup bottles. He turned and drew back his elbow as though he were about to throw it through the bedroom window like a baseball. Men can throw baseballs, Brigid thought. She didn't cower. At the top of the overhand arc, he released and the bottle smashed against the window, cracking it, and clattered to the floor in a crystalline shatter of sea foam and silver porcelain and scented liquid.

He opened the bedroom door and through the doorway the two of them saw Sheila leaving her bathroom, moving quietly in the dim hallway like one of her cats.

He must have met Sheila's gaze. Brigid couldn't see his face but Sheila looked at it long and carefully, and said in a low, measured voice, like someone trying to reason with a small, tired child or a drunk friend, "Would you like me to get someone to drive you home?" He just let out a long breath, a breath with a disgusted laugh underneath it, and pushed past her.

Sheila came in and shut the door. Aren't you proud of me, Sheila? Brigid wanted to say, but instead she cried four short, tearless sobs, like the ones she'd let out when the nurse practitioner had left her alone for a minute to check on something with the doctor after she'd told her that her pregnancy test was positive.

She was still burning from how hard she had done it. She was still slick and wet inside with liquid from him. She would go home and sleep and wake up at three in the afternoon and make coffee and this would still have happened. It would not go away. It was real.

"What did you say to him afterward?" she asked.

"Hey, look out the window," Sheila said.

"What did you say to him?" Brigid asked again.

"I didn't say anything, Brigid," she said. "I didn't say anything to him and he didn't say anything to me. I told you, he never said a word. Look out the window."

"Is it snowing?"

"No, but look, there's frost. It's almost light. There's hardly anybody left downstairs. Your hair's a fucking mess. Want a brush?" She picked one up off the vanity and gave Brigid's hair a stroke or two with it. The early morning outside was silent. No more whoops from the bars, no crackling of the bonfire. Only a scent of stale beer drifted through the dark house.

Brigid put her head down in Sheila's lap and Sheila kept brushing her hair. She thought of saying, I'll go downstairs in a minute. The thing was she didn't want to. She was exhausted. She wanted sleep, only sleep. She lay for a minute letting Sheila stroke her hair with her perfect professional boar-bristled brush and let the feeling of not wanting to say anything seep into her bones. But then she got irritated with Sheila's hands, which were now so gentle on her head. Their softness seemed syrupy sweet, artificial, invasive. She sat up and knocked the brush out of her hand.

As they stared at each other Sheila's eyes got hard. "Brigid, what the fuck did you think? That he'd call you afterward?"

"Fuck you, you bitch," Brigid whispered. Her lungs were tight and dry. "Fuck you. I'm not like you. You lied to me. I never want to see you again."

Sheila stood up. The corners of her mouth drew up in a tiny, tight motion. She gestured toward the door with her hairbrush.

"So leave if you want," she said. "Jesus fucking Christ, I can't tell you what to do, for fuck's sake. Do what you want."

Brigid sat silent on the bed.

"Go on," Sheila said.

Brigid sat still. She was deciding.

Holy Holy Holy

The twelve gates were twelve pearls. The street of
the city was pure gold. And I saw no temple therein.
—*The Revelation of St. John the Divine*

Agatha and her husband, Jasper, do not love me now.
Not since I broke up with Malcolm. We were best friends, we did
everything together. Malcolm needed me, his skinny body and
sleek mind so brilliantly full of algorithms and code searching me
out to comfort him from yet another firing, yet another con-
frontation with a boss who was an idiot. He needed me, so I was
someone who someone else could not do without. And though I
am best out of it, I have become cheerless and awkward and
lonely, with no one there at all. I watch television way too late
into the night, made-for-TV movies starring Bill Bixby and
washed-up child stars, and now that the holidays are upon us,
there are ancient specials too bad to become classics—*The Year
Without a Santa Claus, A Star Wars Christmas*. I watch and nurse
my bad wrist, which wakes me from any sleep I manage.

Agatha and Jasper do not love how transparently needy I
have become, how clingy. But they asked me to their Christmas
party Friday the twenty-third. And by God I was going.

You get carpal tunnel syndrome from working on computers.
I had begun to notice the wrist braces everywhere, more every

day, on receptionists, on tax accountants, on grocery store clerks, canvas and metal and vinyl, like some postapocalyptic white armor. The clerks and receptionists looked at my hand with the recognition of fellow sufferers. "Carpal tunnel?" they would say sympathetically. "Carpal tunnel," I would sigh. When people at work asked how I hurt my wrist I said, "Typing." How absurd. It was unreal; how can you hurt yourself doing something so mundane?

Cassie in customer service, for instance, asked me what I did to my arm when I went down to the fifth floor that Friday afternoon before the party, two days before Christmas. Cassie was my old boss, before I got promoted and started in marketing. I wanted to give her a tin of homemade snowman cookies in shiny red wrapping paper. I leaned into the door of her office as she was showing an inventory printout to the temp. Temps are what we have now; we've laid off a lot of people. I've been spared so far because I've been here a while and I don't whine. There'll be another round of layoffs in January. We'll see.

I held out the tin and they both saw the canvas and metal that stretched from my fingers over the cuff of my cool retro black silk blouse almost to my elbow.

"Honey!" said Cassie. "What happened to your hand?"

I told her all about my carpal tunnel syndrome—the descending stages of tendonitis and repetitive strain injury, nerves rubbed raw by typing memos about our dot-com's sublime and difficult-to-define products, the possibility of surgery to slice open the band of muscle around my wrist. Then I gave her the cookies, kissed her cheek, and said, "Merry Christmas."

"I hate Christmas," murmured Cassie, rolling her eyes. The temp wrinkled her forehead but said nothing.

"I know. I haven't done a thing." I had, but you never say that. "I've got a party to show up at tonight. Have a good holiday, sweetie." I headed for the elevators. Now, when the halls were deserted and dark except for a few fluorescent lights, you could see the more vibrant light of the computer monitors in the cubicles, the glow of their personalized screen savers, spiraling threads and twisting pipes of color and customized scrolling marquees, pictures of greenery and sunsets, slide shows of national parks and surfers seen through electronic windows, flying reindeer for the season, flying toasters for the nostalgic. I downloaded a "Christmas Past" screen saver myself. All black-and-white pictures from the fifties. Kind of cool. Our screens are the logical conclusion of the old toy Lite-Brite, making things with light. I could hear their constant hum. The computers are never turned off. They would hum all through the holidays.

I heard someone walking quickly behind me. It was the temp. She was breathless when she caught up.

"I'm sorry," she said. "I just wanted to talk to you alone, to let you know I wanted to pray for your poor hand."

A picture from school popped into my head. We sat at our hard wooden desks, plaid skirts smooth, white blouses ironed. We raised our hands to ask for special intentions for the Hail Marys that opened every class. "For my father's friend, who just had a heart attack," one girl said. "For a special intention," said someone else. "For the members of Lynyrd Skynyrd who died in the plane crash yesterday," said a bleached blonde. Sister Angelita was never fazed. When she had collected all the intentions she crossed herself in the name of the Father, and of the Son, and of the Holy Spirit and we prayed. Then we did our geometry.

"Oh, that's so sweet of you," I said now to this nice woman. "Thank you. Merry Christmas again." I turned to go.

"Yes, I really wanted to pray for you," she said.

"Yes, thanks," I said.

"It's so important," she continued. "I know the good Lord can help you. I noticed a little room, the one with the microwave and the table, with a door that closes. We wouldn't want anyone to see us."

As I realized that she meant to pray for me *now*, right now, I looked her over more carefully. She was not that much older than me, no more than thirty-five, a plump African-American woman with smooth mahogany skin and a pretty, full face, dressed in a blue suit and pumps with plain pearl earrings in her ears. No big floral Sunday dress or sequined, feathered hat, no raised arms or constant exclamations of "Praise the Lord!"

I thought of Agatha's Christmas party where I was due. All my friends would be there. Agatha's house was so gorgeous. I was lonely, I didn't want to miss any time there, any time among other people who liked me, others who unlike Agatha and her husband, Jasper, had not yet seen my exquisite vulnerability, my weakening ability to cope with the events of my life, my tendency to shatter. I thought of the fire that Jasper would build, of the orange light glowing on the gilt background of the mantelpiece poster they'd brought back from London, the one of the three angels, details from some ancient masterpiece, complete with their harps and halos. Even if Jasper and Agatha loved me no more, there would be good liquor and pine branches and holly on the dark wood banisters and baroque Christmas masses playing on the expensive electronic system. They had a beautiful house, an incredible stereo. They had made a lot of money in the business, as employees six and eight in a startup that did go golden.

"It'll only take a few minutes," the temp said. The thought of explaining to her why I didn't want to bother with this and maybe insulting her made me squirm. And if doctors and casts and braces and cortisone injections couldn't make the pain go away, couldn't stop the lurid ache that woke me at night and the sharp twinges that made me wince when I washed dishes, well, why not? I was scheduled for another shot Christmas Eve day, very early in the morning at the HMO. I hated them—the shots, that is. Of course, I wasn't wild about the HMO, either. Although at least I didn't have to pay the co-payment, because it was worker's comp.

"Um," I said.

"It's just this way." And before I could say "okay" she led me back down the hall to the lunchroom, looking around to see if anyone spotted us. When she closed the lunchroom door she gave a quick, embarrassed smile. I wondered if she was worried about losing her temp spot for this.

She undid all the Velcro fastenings on the brace and very gently stretched out my arm, supporting it with one of her hands while the other lay weightlessly on it. I thought of the time, while flicking through the channels, I'd caught Reverend Jimmy James holding forth about the money the public school system paid to celebrate the satanic holiday of Halloween. Now I stared at the wall of the lunchroom to keep from laughing, but that did no good. What I saw was one of those sequined, embroidered figures of the Virgin of Guadalupe from Mexico. Cassie had brought it back from Cancun and someone had pinned over its head a magazine clipping of the old cartoon character Judy Jetson's face.

Then the temp smiled again, calmly and sweetly.

"Lord," she began, softly, slowly. "Lord, look down on us. Look down on our sister. Lord Jesus, she's in pain. Please help her. Lord, we know you are here. We know you are among us and your power can do anything. We love you and we know that you love us. Please help my sister, please heal her and stop her pain."

My wrist was radiating a funny kind of half-numbness, but I thought it was because I was concentrating so hard on how it felt. I looked at her face. Her eyes were shut and the movements of her lips as she spoke were so small.

I concentrated on the most neutral thing I could look at, her pearl earrings. But then I thought of the pearly gates to heaven in my early schoolbooks. I once heard a woman say, "And there were these magnificent pearl gates," on a TV show about people with near-death experiences. My mind wandered and I wondered if all those pearls were supposed to be white, or if there were supposed to be rare black pearls and honey pearls and those pearls with the pink cast that department store jewelry salesmen say are so complementary to most skin tones. And as I thought of the pearls, the temp began to speak in another language.

I thought at first it was Hebrew but after about a dozen words I realized it wasn't, it didn't have the right sounds, the "ch" sound in "Chanukah" or the singsong rhythm. The words were spoken softly, matter-of-factly. "Leeloma, melo ran dee, lalola, nada far est," she murmured. After a dozen more words she went back to English. The steady pace of her voice was soothing, like a lullaby. The lunchroom was peaceful.

"Thank you, Jesus," she continued. "Thank you, Lord. Yes, we feel your power in this room. We know you are here. Bless us and help us to walk in your footsteps, to love and to heal. Jesus . . . Jesus . . . Jesus . . ." and her voice, which had been so low the whole time, now sank into a whisper. Then she opened her eyes. She was finished.

She looked at me expectantly. We were both silent for a minute.

"It's very calming," I said, because I had to say something.

She nodded enthusiastically. "Yes, it is calming, the Lord's presence."

I stretched my hand, flexing the wrist, experimenting with turning it different ways. "Does it feel any better?" she asked anxiously.

"Not yet," I confessed. I hated to disappoint her. I was oddly disappointed myself. But the sharp pain still jolted through me whenever I so much as wiggled my fingers.

But she wasn't disappointed. "It'll feel better later tonight," she said. "After you've been home a few hours."

"Yes, maybe it will. I'll watch for it."

"I know it will," she answered. I had been thinking how funny Cassie would find all this when I told her about it. But now I decided I wouldn't.

I put the brace back on, not knowing how to leave. "Thank you," I said. "Really, thank you. And Merry Christmas." I gave her a quick hug and kissed her cheek. She had, after all, been kind.

"And Merry Christmas to you," she said. I turned the knob on the lunchroom door. She stayed there.

I had to wait a long time for the elevator because the building maintenance man had turned off all but one of them for the holiday. I listened to the piped-in carols while I waited, which I liked better than the usual office easy listening. I could hear words I had never heard before, the second and third verses to the songs, the Latin version of "O Come All Ye Faithful," the parts everyone mumbles because they don't know them.

I parked my old silver Honda—it looked Christmasy, the silver next to the white snow—half a block from Agatha's warm windows. They glowed so yellow against the cold and the night and the thick, icy stars. Through the panes I could see the roomful of handsome people, the glasses in their hands sparkling in the firelight, and above the mantel the gilded poster. I had forgotten the angels were wearing wreaths of white roses topped with pearl crowns in their hair and held their heads bowed to sing the praises of God. In the night they looked beautiful to me, beckoning. As I got to the door I heard Renaissance Christmas music. Agatha had tacked a spray of those hard little mistletoe berries on the top of the door frame. Snow frosted the pine trees on either side of the front steps.

Agatha and Jasper got me a drink and I sat by the fire next to the Christmas tree, Agatha's Christmas tree so tastefully hung with antique ornaments, an aged and faded star studded with yellowed pearls, glass beads in silver and white and gold strung through the branches. There would be no ugly, cheerful, cheap tinsel in this home. The white fluffy cat Karma jumped in my lap. People asked me how my day had been and I told them about the temp, the prayer, the foreign words.

"She was *speaking in tongues?*" said Jasper.

I shrugged. "Yeah."

"You went into a room alone with an evangelical maniac?" he said.

"She was only trying to help."

When the story—a good party story, I still have to admit, like my Catholic school tales—had been told for everyone who had missed it and eventually all lost interest, the rocking Christmas music came on, Phil Spector, Chuck Berry, Springsteen's "Santa

Claus Is Coming to Town." We formed a conga line and, drunk and warm, we kicked and hopped and then we jostled the Christmas tree so that the rich loops of golden beads swayed. One of the red glass balls fell and shattered in that tinkly way they do. I looked at the antique star balanced at the top, dipping dangerously.

And as I looked up at the star, it swayed too far to one side. I arched up to save it but I only made it worse, it swung with the branches and I could tell it would fall, in a split second the gold glass and yellowed pearls would be all over the floor, smashed, and I saw it for a single moment suspended by a thread of wire and then it was over, not just the star but the whole tree with its strings of tiny beads descended, floating downward on the air, and hit the polished golden brown floor with the massive smack of a tree falling in the forest. The star split into its many delicate splinters, the pearls from it rolled across the floor, the silvery strings unraveled and snaked their way toward the dining room, and even as we thought that would be the end of it and Agatha was going for the dustpan, the ceiling seemed to open up, like floodgates, and a hundred thousand, a thousand thousand pearls rained down on us. White and cream and black and ivory and silver-gray they were, tiny seed pearls and big ones like out of cocktail rings. They clattered across the hardwood floor, bounced off our noses, and fell down the backs of our necks. They fell into the dip and skipped off the CDs. They hid themselves amid the lazy bubbles of sparkling water going flat in beer tumblers and nestled like tiny shining eggs in the dust bunnies under the sofa. They rolled under our feet and some of us slipped on them and fell, arms flailing, and did not rise again. Karma the cat galloped off in terror. They kept coming, thousands of them, a hard blizzard of pearls, the clicking of each little orb and pellet coming together into a thunderous, rolling din, like Niagara Falls, difficult to see through, impossible to hear over. And all around me the wide eyes turned to stare as if I had somehow brought this thing with me, ushered it in through the door.

One fell into my crystal champagne glass. I took it out and held it, pale pink and luminous, between my thumb and first finger. The din stopped, the downpour was over, and the sudden silence roared in our ears. I ran from the room, through the elegant hall, out the door, and stopped on the front steps. In the evening dark the pine trees loomed up, soft and black. The white necklaces of snow gleamed on the branches. And there I sat down and wept.

February 14

Hail, Bishop Valentine, whose day this is;
all the air is thy diocese.

John Donne, upon hearing of the
marriage of his friends on Valentine's Day

I have always liked that quote. Senior honors literature with Sister Veronica, all those years ago.

1

February 1953. Sister Veronica at the bottom of the gymnasium stairs with the bar of soap to wash our faces with if she caught us wearing rouge or lipstick. In the drugstore on the way home, where we buy the rouge and the lipstick, packets of die-cut valentines, in shapes, for children. The paper skunk, below his feet in two linked hearts the words "Valentine—I'm scent-imental about you!" And the bowl of salad. "You bowl me over, lettuce be valentines." Memories even farther back, of a schoolroom party with Coca-Cola sipped through straws we made by biting the ends off red licorice, of a box covered with red construction paper, of these shapely bits of card in white envelopes slid through the slot in the top, of the count of how many each of us had. We were all supposed to bring one for everyone if we brought any at all, but pretty girls and cute boys always got more. And there was one in each package of valentines especially for teacher. That sad, sad basset hound, in the heart above his head, "Will you flea with me, teacher? Be my valentine!" Today, of course, manufacturers do not waste the time or paper. Valentines for children are perforated, and square, in sheets, every one in the package with a prefabricated Disney character, a pink princess. Six to a sheet.

II

I am an old woman now, alone again. I take long walks every day, watch the birds and the changing foliage. A senior citizen's pleasures.

There is a house of men on my street, on the corner near the train station. I see it every day. A very old man, much, much older than me, wizened and gray, sits on the porch in the afternoon even in great silver rain showers and listens to opera. He is the only man I ever see there. But I know, I just know, they're inside.

The house is flat-roofed and square with two levels, the top one slightly smaller, like a pagoda, with the stairs painted red for good luck. The tiny garden in front has been designed so that something is blooming in it no matter what time of year it is. It looks best in the summer rain, with the pink and yellow roses and the warm crystal all over the grass. I know it's a house of men because I know the souls of all *my* men, all the ones I have ever loved, live there. The old one takes care of them. I see him calming their many anxieties with soothing wisdom. I see them swigging Buds in front of the preseason football games, like my father and older brothers and husband, all gone now, and talking about changing brake pads. Even the ones who don't like football are fitting in somehow, writing poetry over black coffee, like the ones who so captured and twisted my heart in my two years of college, where I went to find my husband. I see them going into dinner in two straight lines, breaking their bread, brushing their teeth, going to bed.

III

This place in my mind is 1953, and I'm at the drugstore.

"Bishop," I say in front of the greeting card display, "are you an ornament?"

He says he is Valentine, patron saint of lovers.

He is the candy.

He is the red lace.

He is the heart-shaped box.

Valentine, says Sister Veronica in class, was probably Bishop of Terni, martyred in Rome in the third century. No one knows how he became the saint associated with love, although there is a story that he helped young lovers exchange messages, notes, the first valentine cards. She tells us that when he prostrated himself before God he said, "I am a heart.

"The love flashes hot and golden and my knees buckle.

"I can't stop it any more than I can stop the ocean. It's like the ocean; it can destroy with a little of its own extra excitement the brittle things we build and call solid.

"I am its vessel. Pray for me. Have mercy on *me*, Lord."

Valentine, patron of lovers. My lovers. My young daughter's lovers. All lovers.

IV

The man who seems to live on the train platform calls out to me from under his wild hair. On his red T-shirt is printed only "John 11:35." Big block white letters ironed on. He must be very cold. I need my wool coat wrapped tightly around me.

John 11:35 is the shortest verse in the Bible. *Jesus wept.*

The man calls out to me, "Jesus didn't weep, he sobbed. His body convulsed in great wails, his chest and lungs and throat closed up with suffering." A little crowd begins to gather around him, around both of us, staring at him, staring at me as if I know him.

"He choked on his loneliness; he tore up the ground with spastic, digging hands and rubbed the dirt in his hair. The apostles were frightened and would not go near him in his hysteria. He cried because he knew he was abandoned and felt so ugly and ashamed. What a desolate fate: the love poured from him like Niagara and nobody wanted it."

V

I have the time and the modest means, so I travel. The chance that I so dreamed of long ago, to see the world, has come. I take full advantage of the Silver Series Seniors' Tours. It might have been better to go when my knees were stronger and I could hike for hours with all my worldly goods in a backpack, instead of needing a whole separate bag for my heart medicine and my thyroid medication and my hormone replacement therapy, but I do not complain. I am lucky to be able to afford it, to still have the health at my age to go. And, while the group is following the guide in some exotic locale, I often slip away on my own for a time.

There is one place I have never been. Can you imagine?

"Watch your heads, everyone, as we pass through the aortic valve," the guide would say. "It's a tight squeeze. We're now entering the cavern.

"Has everyone got a lantern? Can we all stand up? We didn't lose anyone? Fine. Now then. To your right, the right ventricle; to your left, the left ventricle. Observe the smoothness of the walls. The erosion caused by years of blood flow. Note the contrast with the scarred outer muscle we saw earlier. Yes? Question? Oh, no, the scarring is a perfectly normal part of the aging process.

"Watch it, watch it, watch it! Step back, everyone, quickly! Were some of you splashed? I'm so sorry. That's the way it is, you know. We're dealing with nature. That bloody tide rushes through very powerfully every second. Observe the heightened temperature and color of the inner wall.

"Can you all hear that? That muffled, rhythmic drumbeat? It regulates the process, originating in the organ itself, separate from nervous system control. Even fragments of cardiac muscle in a tissue culture will continue to contract rhythmically.

"Look around you. Yes, you may raise your lanterns. Observe carefully. These are the inner workings of the functioning human heart."

VI

In a Thai city I saw the Temple of the Emerald Buddha. The Buddha is not large and the theory is that it is made of jade or some kind of marcasite. It has a long history of loss and restoration, like the Hope Diamond.

The king who built the temple a hundred and fifty years ago fought a war, Helen-of-Troy style, to rescue his queen from abductors. He loved to collect European art, though he had Eastern art, too. He collected the Buddha for his queen. In the same room with it are seventeenth-century Italian cherubs with rosebud mouths and little bows and arrows. I wonder how an Eastern king knew to put those Western gods there, for love?

VII

In Prague I take a moment to sit in a pew in the Chapel of Saint Agnes, which is called the Chapel of Mirrors, in the church called the Klementina. It's the Chapel of Mirrors because there are mirrors in it, which my Silver Series literature says is unusual in a house of God. Silver-backed glass is inlaid in bands across the ceiling and panels in the wall above the gilt wainscoting. Everything is all lacy effluvia, rose and mauve and curling woodwork. This place was built to honor Saint Agnes, one of the virgin martyrs, in fact the patron saint of virgins. Her feast day is January 21. They say that if unmarried girls perform certain rituals on Saint Agnes's Eve, they'll dream of their future husbands.

Agnes, Sister Veronica told us, refused to marry a Roman soldier and as punishment she was "exposed" in a brothel, where she healed a soldier who had been struck blind upon attempting to violate her. They are always in pictures of her. The eyes, that is. They're usually growing out of a vine she holds. It's quite eerie.

Saint Agnes, poor raped teenager that you probably were—what do these sugar pink walls and golden angels and silver mirrors have to do with you? What's all this froth to you? What are we doing here, you and me, in this room of glass?

VIII

1973. My daughter is wailing and it pierces my heart. He hasn't called. He hasn't called. Everything was fine and then *he just stopped calling.*

"Oh, baby," I say. "They do that sometimes."

"Why?"

"I don't know, baby." We all simply accepted it.

She looks at me, then at the room in general. "Gentlemen. I address you!" she calls. She was always dramatic. *"What's the deal?"*

When she is at school—she goes in jeans and puts her uniform skirt on at her locker when she gets there, we never would have dared—I dutifully listen to some of her music, to understand her better. *Jesus Christ Superstar.* What would Sister Veronica have said? It's rather rousing.

IX

1986. My daughter married, my husband two years dead. My daughter says, "Go for it, Mom!" so I have dinner with the nice man from church. Everything is fine and then he just stops calling.

I get a shock when my daughter tells me that Sister Veronica is still teaching religion, that refuge for fading nuns, at the school where some of her friends' children go. But of course, I think, why shouldn't she? In high school I thought of her as so distantly middle-aged but now with a start I realize she is probably only ten years older than I am.

X

On my walk, past the train station and back, by the house of my men, the last of the winter holly glows dark red and shiny gloss green against its own woody twigs. A young woman, her face Chinese, her clothes and manner American, is stacking boxes outside. I stop and gaze.

She notices me and I am certainly unthreatening, an aging woman smiling across the cold lawn, so she smiles at me weakly, and I say, "I do always love this garden. Is it your father who sits out here so often?"

Her smile grows broader but more wistful. "It was," she says. "It was his garden. He's passed away."

The emptiness, the woodenness inside me. "I'm so sorry."

"Thank you." She turns to go inside, get more boxes.

I walk on. The drugstore. Tonight is a holy night. The feast of Saint Valentine.

I buy shining red stars, glitter and cherry-colored ribbons, packs of playing cards, pencils in pink and bronze. Bought out the whole store.

At home, deep in Valentine's night, inside my immaculate and tasteful house, I make a gigantic valentine. I take out all the kings and queens of hearts and throw the rest of the packs away. Cover squares of red paper with all my silver and gold and luster, with fans of the cardboard royalty, glitter to evoke the universe and all its planets and celestial bodies. As fast as I can I glue on pictures of diamonds and rubies from magazines. I don't know what it is yet but I know it's out there, my love is there, somewhere. It's time.

I tie the valentine all up with shining satin ribbons.

At dawn I go through the town, past the train station to the bay, to the mailbox on Waterfront Street. As I walk down I see on the pier an early-morning swimmer, like a seal in his slick, dark wetsuit. He dives off the railing. I look for him in the waves, but I don't see him.

At the mailbox I tear the valentine into a thousand glittering red and white pieces and throw them into the air. The wind swirls and picks them up, carries them past the bay, past the train station, past John 11:35, past the house of men. I toss red and white roses after the pieces, and they swirl away, too, in white bubbling whirlwinds, and I ask him, you know, the king of hearts, king of the air and the water, to send my valentine away and return it to me transformed into love. To work it through the tides, through the ocean, through the breezes and the windstorms, to push it up through the earth, circle it all around back to me. I can feel it beginning, warm, an oval made between the entrance to my body and the earth. I can feel them tied together, and I know that this valentine will come back to me. No matter that I'm afraid that it will, no matter that I'm afraid that it won't. Bishop Valentine, like a softer Reaper, is coming for me again.

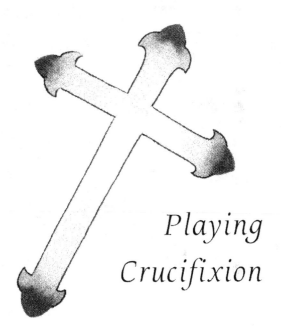

Playing
Crucifixion

Christine and Emmy, seventeen, were swinging on the playground swings one Sunday afternoon in very late winter. There had been an unseasonable thaw and there were little buds on the trees that were probably going to die soon but that shimmered a pretty baby green in the sun anyway. A very young man, a boy really, surprised them by coyly saying "Hi" from where he stood behind the bushes that bordered one edge of the park.

Christine took it coolly. She gradually stopped swinging. She was hard to faze, and Emmy envied her for it. Christine was no older but far fewer things surprised her. They were both young to be college freshmen. One of the first things they found they had in common, besides that they had both come to this fine brick and greenery campus from families with no money, was that they had each skipped a grade in school. This had happened to Emmy because she was shy and studious, but Christine was bohemian and intellectual. Her dad was a professor—hence her scholarship—and she had gone to the lab school on campus. Her life had included reading assignments straight from Freud, teenage ménages à trois, trips to Switzerland that left her speaking French and German fluently, and owning a wardrobe of long, exotic scarves and calf-high boots.

She looked at the boy through the tiny glasses perched on her beaky nose.

"Are you tripping?" she asked. And Emmy looked at his glowing eyes and saw what Christine had seen, the fine, thin rim of blue iris around his pupil, which was wide and shining even in the bright sunlight. She wished she had thought to ask that. He grinned shyly and looked down, pretending to be sheepish.

"I thought so," said Christine. He was so cute, with his printed pajama top thrown over a dark blue T-shirt, and with his rumpled hair. He didn't seem cold, and of course it *was* warmer than usual, but Emmy and Christine still needed their peacoats. Emmy wondered if they had seen him before, at a frat party last night, or the night before last. Or maybe not. She had certainly met a dozen boys who looked something like him in the last few months. Not a one of them had wanted her. Christine told her she tried too hard, but how else could you try when you wanted something? She didn't understand why it was so difficult to get what she wanted, such a small thing. A boyfriend, that was all. Someone to hold her all night, whispering, cajoling, someone she could sweetly, shyly refuse until she finally gave in and he poured his gratitude all over her.

The boy looked at them for a minute. Then he said, "I just lost my job, is the thing. So I thought tripping might cheer me up."

Emmy thought of something to say. "Did we meet you last night? At Kappa Sigma?"

"I don't know," he said, shrugging. His eyes focused on Christine, and Emmy felt stupid and decided not to venture any more questions. Christine told her she was too shy, she should just be herself. "You're the one they always look at, for Christ's sake," she said. Christine, though tall and slim, was geeky, sleek but not pretty. Emmy was more nubile, brown-haired, a girl next door. And she was too ashamed to tell Christine how used she had gotten to getting the attention of young males and then blowing it by saying something awkward. She thought she made them feel awkward, too.

She had been ashamed in exactly the same way the night in her dorm room that Christine recounted the story of how she had lost her virginity to a vulgar French teenager.

"When did you?" she had asked Emmy.

Emmy had considered lying. Someone as clever as Christine, though, could have found her out some time or other, caught her saying something as she tried to be light and silly that revealed her inexperience. So she had said, "I haven't yet," looking down, and endured Christine's no comment and raised eyebrows.

"So why'd you lose your job?" Christine asked now. Oh, that, thought Emmy. Now, that's what I should have said.

He sat down cross-legged in the dirt in front of the swings while the girls dangled their feet on the ground, lightly swaying back and forth.

"Well, I work in this day-care center. The child development place in the lab school. I mean, worked."

"I know that place," said Christine.

Emmy thought that he looked like someone kids would like, all smiles and pajama top, like someone parents could trust their children with, despite the fact that he was currently on acid. Christine liked acid. Emmy was developing a light taste for it, too.

"And?" Christine pressed.

He looked up at her, smiled. "And I got fired for teaching the little kids to play Crucifixion."

"Excuse me?"

"They loved it," he said, stretching his legs out in the dirt. "No, really."

"How do you play? It sounds weird."

He laughed. "I get them all to yell 'Crucify him! Crucify him!'" He smiled broadly and buried his head in his shoulder for a second, like a bird grooming its wing. He couldn't quite keep his body or his face still.

"And then they all form a mob, and they drag me over to the monkey bars"—he spread out his arms and fell backward onto the cold, hard ground—"and they hold me there, and I say, you know, 'It is finished,' all that stuff. Until the bell rings."

Emmy tried to picture it. Him in his pajama top, roughhousing with a bunch of little kids. There'd be nursery-school teacher types glancing out the window at recess, watching him, smiling at the children. At first it would just seem like they were playing something commonplace, ring-around-the-rosy or something. Then it would start to look strange. The teachers would wonder why he was being led over to the monkey bars. Then they'd watch with increasing horror while the kids, laughing, climbed all over his cruciform arms and legs like swarming grasshoppers and he called out, "It is finished."

The boy sat up suddenly and arranged his face so it looked serious and intense, wrinkling his forehead and frowning. "Hey, do you want to take a walk with me? I want to show you something."

"Sure," said Christine, hopping off the swing.

He only looked at Emmy briefly. She had been so proud, lately, of being open to unusual things. Of taking acid and tripping in darkened rooms, of the dark underground caverns where she had gone to see thrashing bands, of the cheeses and chocolates and wine Christine taught her to shop for, of spontaneous midnight walks full of discussions of fate and free will. She hopped off her swing, too.

"What's your name?" Christine said to him.

"Jack."

He opened the gate to the wooden fence around the playground and they went through, heading back toward school.

The campus was old and impressive, full of secret little niches and forgotten antiques. Christine and Emmy had once found a pair of real red velvet Victorian love seats abandoned on the landing of a decrepit office building. They had climbed through a trapdoor another time and come up in a tiny theater decorated with Greco-Roman friezes at the top of one of the lecture buildings. Emmy thought they must be heading toward something like that.

Jack walked ahead of them across the dead winter lawns and stone paths. It was midafternoon and the sun was getting warm and harshly bright.

"I went there," said Christine, pointing to a gray brick building they passed that had trailers used as classrooms parked in front. "That's lab."

"Did you?" said Jack. He glanced over at the building, and then he stood on his hands and started walking on them. His back arched so that his feet went way over his head and his face turned bright red almost immediately.

"Did *you*?" asked Emmy. He seemed like a lab school product. Maybe Christine wouldn't have known him if he'd been far enough ahead of her.

"No," he grunted. "I went to boarding school. The Sather School. Know it?"

Christine nodded but Emmy was blank. "What was it like?" Emmy asked.

Jack let his feet drop to the ground, stood up, and did a couple of cartwheels before he answered.

"Everyone had a *horse*," he said, in a definite way. "There was a joke my sophomore year. People would say, 'If Jack helped you off a horse, would you help Jack off a horse?' So my nickname was 'me off' for a while."

"That's funny," said Christine in the dry voice Emmy liked so much to hear her use with other people.

Jack turned to Emmy. "Did *you* go to boarding school?"

"No," she said, surprised by the question.

"It's just like college," said Jack. "But I like my roommate now better. His name is Mack. So everybody in the dorm calls us both 'Ack.' That's funny, too." He spun his head toward Christine.

"Yup," she said, and Emmy saw her staring appreciatively at his blue and black shining eyes. They went on.

There was a fork in one of the paths and he stopped for a minute, for the first time looking a little confused. "This way," he said after a second, pointing to the left. He turned to make sure they were following. Emmy had held her eyes fixed on his back, so when he turned he caught her gaze. He winked.

Emmy had a flash of memory. She had seen a wink just like

that not long ago. It was the wink of the pilot who had flown the plane she had taken to school. She happened to be right behind him as she boarded. She was tired from getting up early and she had gazed absently at his back. The pilot turned and saw her doing it, caught her eye. Automatically she readied herself for the response she hadn't yet realized she had come to expect over the last few years when men on the street or the bus or at the mall caught her eye—the stare, the leer, the comment, the pursed lips. The laughter, real or silent, at her embarrassment. Sometimes they even winked.

But this pilot's wink wasn't like that. It was a confident, knowing, safe wink. The wink of an uncle. The wink of a father. A wink that said, "Don't you worry, young lady. I'll get this plane up and down safe. You just watch the movie." A wink with no sex in it, no sex at all. As though he didn't notice that she was a teenager, almost a woman. There was such comfort in that wink. It seemed she hadn't seen one like it in a long time.

She was spacing, and she must have been staring absently at Jack. He said, "What? What are you thinking?"

"About my dad," she answered.

"Your dad?" He started to walk on tiptoe on the very edge of the path where the grass met the paving stones, holding his arms out for balance. "Dads. What's your dad do?"

"He manages a shoe store," she said.

"Shoes? That's nice. That's nice," he said. "My dad, my dad's an investment analyst."

"Wow," said Emmy, aware that Christine was watching them with faint amusement—her quiet little answers, his flailing for balance on the stones.

"You want to know what he told me?" he asked.

"What?"

"He said I was a bad investment."

"Oh," said Emmy. Then, "I'm sorry."

He shrugged. "Hey, what's your roommate like?"

"Umm . . ." Emmy giggled. "Well, actually she's a born-again

Christian." She was. Emmy slept on the floor in Christine's single room a lot just to get away from her.

"No!" He smiled. "Really?"

"Yeah. And she's anorexic, too. I think. She never eats. She did the Kappa Sig muscular dystrophy dance-a-thon to lose weight. She prays for me a lot."

He laughed. "That's great. That's great." He gave up on his balancing act and they walked on for a time in silence, him still ahead. Christine grabbed Emmy's arm to get her to fall back a little.

"God, he's so cute!" she whispered.

"I knew you'd think so." Emmy smiled. She liked to be a little knowing with Christine.

"He seems kind of oblivious, though," Christine muttered, wrinkling her forehead. She skipped forward and called, "Wait up!" Emmy could hear her making her voice light, teasing. Christine gripped Jack's elbow and stepped along with him. This was a habit she had picked up in Europe, where schoolgirls walked arm-in-arm all the time. She did it with Emmy a lot. She turned and waved at Emmy to speed up, motioned for her to get on the other side of him. It would have been a nice picture, Emmy thought, him in the middle, a girl on each arm. But she kept her hands in her pockets. She was comfortable in the mood his wink had put her in. When she looked at his forearm and his knobby wrist sticking out from his sleeve, she thought that if she touched him, she might spoil it.

"Well, I'm glad I found you guys," he said, looking up at the sun and squinting. "I'd probably have just wandered around looking at the broken glass glittering in the street."

"Isn't this more fun?" asked Christine, squeezing his arm.

"Yeah. Yeah, wait. Here." He turned off the stone path to a trail marked only by some dead grass that was more trodden down than usual. There were trees on either side of the trail, and a tiny bridge over a stream.

He led them to the back entrance of the old Hall of Science.

It was run-down, small, practically unheated, and covered with dead ivy, but it was built out of solid stone and wasn't crumbling yet. It was only used for an odd graduate seminar now, not for regular lecture classes or labs.

There was a great slash cut in the cyclone fence behind the building. He stepped through it. "Careful," he said in a low voice, like he was in a library. The lock on the hall's old metal side door was taped over so it wouldn't close. Jack smiled as he turned the knob. It didn't make a sound, not even a click.

The floor was an old institutional green linoleum. The light came from a giant skylight. The brass-colored grillwork on the banisters was too old to shine as the sun touched it.

He led them up one flight of stairs. "So where are we going?" asked Christine.

"Just up here," he said.

Behind his shoulders, Emmy looked at Christine and gave a tiny shake of her head. Christine nodded, then shrugged to show she thought it was okay. Emmy knew that going off with boys one didn't know could be dangerous. She hadn't expected to be led somewhere so deserted. "He doesn't *seem*—you know?" Christine murmured in her ear.

"I know," said Emmy. Christine giggled, her eyes on Jack's butt.

He heard the giggle. "Just one more," he called. He had cleared the second staircase and they started up after him.

"Where?" asked Christine sharply.

"Okay, okay, just a second. Up *here*. Jeez," he muttered, then laughed. He turned around to face them at the top of the third staircase, right beneath the skylight, and pointed.

At the end of the narrow corridor was a window. He walked toward it awkwardly, shuffling his feet, his hands stuffed in the pockets of his jeans. Christine and Emmy followed.

Arranged in two rows on the right side of the window were twelve black-and-white photographs of young men in leather flight helmets and sheepskin jackets. Their names were written on the lower edges of the frames. A plain brass plaque under the pictures read "In memory of the members of the class of 1944 who, called by their country, made the Supreme Sacrifice." In smaller type beneath these words it said "The Class of 1946."

"I like to come up here sometimes," he said. "I have kind of an, I don't know, kind of an affinity for this guy." He pointed to the second one from the left in the top row. Captain John Robert Flynn. "I think I look like him, a little." He cast down his eyes modestly, then brought them back up again. "What do you think?"

He did look like him. He really did. Not every single feature, but right in the eyes there was definitely a similarity. And in the grin.

Emmy stepped closer to stare at the picture. She said, "Yeah, you do. Wow. I mean, you do."

"Yeah," he said. "So I like to come up here and kind of hang out with him for a while."

"When you're tripping?" chirped Christine.

"Sometimes," he answered, looking at the picture, not her. "Other times, too. Just in the middle of the day, sometimes. Or at night. Doesn't matter."

They were all silent for a second, looking at Captain John Robert Flynn. Then Jack shook himself from his shoulders to his toes and turned to leave. Christine started to follow him, but Emmy stayed where she was, her forehead wrinkled, her eyes surprised. Jack turned back.

"What?" he asked. He took a step toward her, looked intently at her face. "What?"

"I smell leather," she said. She looked up at him. "I smell . . . leather jackets."

He nodded. "Yeah," he said.

He turned and clopped down the stairs and Emmy and Christine followed. When they got out the door and reached the cyclone fence behind the building, they sank down with their backs to it as though they had all agreed to rest. Jack picked up a couple of sticks and pretended to do a drumroll on the ground.

"Well, it was cool," said Christine. He didn't answer. His eyes were closed and he was whistling.

Giggling, Christine stretched her leg over both of his to play footsie with Emmy, while he leaned back his head to get the sun on his face and otherwise didn't move, even though Christine lightly kicked him.

Suddenly he threw away the sticks, stood up, and slammed his back against the fence. It rang with the impact of his body. He stretched out his arms wide and as Emmy stared at him he caught her eye and smiled knowingly, flirtingly. It was at that moment, that precise second, that Emmy became intensely, sharply aware that she still hadn't touched him.

"Let's play Crucifixion!" he cried. "C'mon!"

Christine laughed. "No handcuffs," she said, motioning to his wrists. "Nothing to tie you up there with."

"Aw, do what the kids do," he said. He shrugged, raised his eyebrows, and kept his hands stretched out, his fingers spread against the interlocking wires of the fence.

"Crucify me!" he called out, smiling and interrupting himself with laughter.

Christine grabbed one of his wrists. She circled it with her two hands, sticking her fingers through the fence and wrapping them around his forearm, holding on as hard as she could, trying to pin him.

Emmy, watching, reached out to touch his other wrist. His skin was warm, which she had thought it would be, but it was also smooth, like a child's, which surprised her. This close to him she realized he smelled sweet, like fresh flannel. She wrapped her fingers around him the way that Christine had, and braced herself to hold him there.

"Okay, okay," he said. He closed his eyes and rolled his head from side to side. "Okay, I'm dying now. Okay. I'm thirsty. I need a Coke. My Lord, my Lord, why have you forgotten me? Yeah, everybody can come hang out with me in heaven . . . okay, okay . . . it's finished. It's all over." He sighed. His head was turned toward Emmy and he opened his eyes and winked at her. "I think I'm dead," he whispered so only she could hear, and she burst out laughing. He smiled and shut his eyes again.

"Okay, okay," he said again. "I'm dead now. You gotta let me down."

"No!" said Christine, teasing. He let his eyes rest on her.

"Nope, you gotta take me down. You gotta do the Pietà thing. Okay?"

They looked at each other.

"So on the count of three, let go," he said. They nodded. He solemnly counted. "One . . . two . . ." He dragged out the two. "Two and a half!" he called gleefully. And then, in a deep voice, "Three!"

They let go and Jack waved his arms back and forth, pretending to be off balance. "Whoa! Whoa!" he cried, and then he pitched forward, headed straight toward the sidewalk, and Emmy tried to break his fall, and at the last second he veered toward her anyway, and fell with all his weight into her arms. But she caught him, and she fell backwards, and he was on top of her. And she felt him, and she had never felt anything, anything, like the heaviness of his body before, the weight of this boy in her arms. She felt the strength of the long muscle that formed the front of his thigh, and his hand with its fingers spread on her back through her shirt, and the back of his neck where her fingers rested, and the down on the back of that neck, and his breath against her ear, and the fabric of his pajama top, and his hard kneecap where it banged hers, and she smelled his hair, and she didn't know what to do, how to move, where to put herself. Where's Christine? she thought vaguely. She must be here somewhere. And then that disappeared because she didn't care, although she was scared for not caring, she felt like there had been some mistake and she had somehow cheated Christine of something, and was an ungrateful friend, forgetting about her. She was stiff, and she hated it, because either Jack's hands or his legs or his mouth, she didn't know which, had pressed her somewhere that opened some secret sliding panel in her, like in a Chinese puzzle box. What do you want, what do you need? she thought. I'll give you anything you need, anything. Only tell me what it is. I'll give you my warmth, I'll give you my mouth, I'll give you my breath. Then she stopped and wondered, Is that love? Is what I just thought love?

With his arms around her, Jack stood up and pulled Emmy to her feet. He didn't dust himself off. With him still holding her she turned her head so she could say something in his ear. "Oh, God damn it," she tried to whisper, but it came out almost a hiss because she was so anxious that her voice, even so soft, couldn't be tender. "Want me. Want *me.*"

"Oh, I know," he said into her neck. "I know." He put his hands on the back of her head. He made her lay it on his shoulder and touched her hair, over and over, with his fingertips. Then the fingertips ran all over whatever he could reach, her shoulders, the back of her thighs, and after a second's pause, slipped into the back pockets of her jeans and pressed her up against him. She could still feel him, still heavy, still leaning on her some, but now she felt his legs, his thighs, his whole being, pushing into her. She felt his sinews and the cuts of his muscles, hard and strong because of his youth, beneath his clothes. He wasn't there to stay. She knew he would hold her until the moment passed. She raised her head to look at him, and though he did not release her, his glowing eyes were already shifting to look at the green trees behind her. Sometime this afternoon, she knew, and probably not very far from now, he would walk away, back into them. But she shook anyway.

Merry Christmas,
Charlie Brown

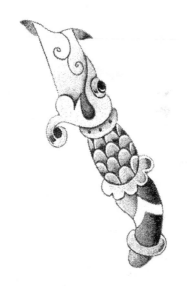

Molly is standing in her room drying her hair. She's glad to be going out because her roommate Liberty is at work, and she is all alone in the house with Liberty's new knives.

Liberty's gourmet set of task-specific blades is lovely. There are paring knives, carving knives, serrated bread cutters, tomato corers, small and large butchers' cleavers, all arranged in a wooden block on the kitchen counter. Their smooth black handles stick up in a perfect graduated row, cascading from largest to smallest. It is the Saturday before Christmas, and Liberty will be gone all day cooking at the Royal Café. Maybe she'll pull overtime.

Molly has been careful not to let anyone know, to wear long sleeves, but of late when she is by herself with a knife in her hand, she has taken to dragging it across her wrists and the insides of her forearms. She usually uses the X-Actos from the studio at school. She is an architecture student and she's at the studio a lot to finish her models and drawings. It's a hard master's program and she works late at night. It's easy to be alone. Sometimes she gently scratches the skin over her heart, or she holds the glittering blade behind her head and with it traces her spine between her shoulder blades. Sometimes she breaks the firm, satiny surface of her skin and sometimes she doesn't. So far, that is as far as it has gone. But in the last week or so she has wanted to keep going, to draw all over her body, elaborate patterns of flowing lines, spirals and curlicues, detailed, feathery designs like the ones Jack Frost carves on windowpanes. In her mind's eye she sees the silver knife dragging along her thigh, leaving indelibly in its wake a beautiful curling vine. And deeper, of course, she is always tempted to go deeper, to hit and unleash the gush of red. That would make the thready wounds even more real, and she would be one step closer to eternal relaxation, to sleep.

Someday, Molly thinks, looking in the mirror and holding the blow dryer under her hair, I'll slice my face and then people will see. I won't be able to help it. She imagines the drops of blood like tears rolling down her clear cheeks. Then, she thinks, they'll know all about it. Then they'll lock me up.

Still looking at herself, she buries her hands in her hair, her fingertips spread out around the crown of her head. Before she knows she is doing it, she has sunk her nails into her scalp. Horrified, she snatches her hands away from herself and cries out as though she has seen a spider. But within her fear she feels a soft relief, as though a waterfall of tension has been released from her temples. What is it? she mouths to the mirror. What is wrong? It is opaque to her, but she knows it's there, formless, behind the mirror, behind her own mind's front door.

There is no more than the usual traumatic childhood to cause this, Molly thinks to herself, no more than the mundane dysfunction of a hundred thousand other children of her century. Or, she wonders, is what is happening to her genetic, like hemophilia, the disease that makes small boys bleed forever? Or perhaps like multiple sclerosis, lying dormant, striking viciously in young adulthood?

"No." She says it aloud. Molly does not accept that anything about her could be particularly dramatic. She has never felt destined for either greatness or tragedy, and she thinks she would sense it in her bones somehow if she were. But she does not understand why God or fate or whatever has chosen her from among all her peers, some far more qualified, to manifest her world's gasps of exhaustion and sadness and abandonment. It's not that she wants this lot to fall to anyone else—she's pleased to spare other people pain—but she does wish it didn't have to fall to her. Suffering is universal, she knows. But she also knows that no one will see her new habit from her point of view.

"I'm scared," she says to the mirror, "of what they'll think." How gradual, she wonders, is madness? What are the symptoms and where are the lines? Her sanity is the only home she has.

She hurries to get out of the house and among people before another urge to lacerate wells up within her. The world is so full of sharp objects.

She's meeting Sam tonight. Sam is an old boyfriend. Molly likes keeping up with old boyfriends. It makes her feel like a good person to recognize the value and sweetness of men who, for one reason or another, couldn't stay with her.

The night is cold but dry and Molly is warm enough in her jeans and big turtleneck and ripped sweater. The Touch, the bar where she's meeting Sam, is right across from the old movie house and next door to a florist, on a block of University that's full of record stores and bakeries and newsstands. Sunflowers, Christmas roses, holly, and mistletoe spill out of the buckets beneath the florist's awning, and over them drift the carols from the tough old weathered radio by the cash register. "Hark! the herald angels sing, Glory to the newborn King. Peace on Earth, and mercy mild, God and sinners reconciled." Everything is strung with tasteful white lights and this is calming to Molly, the warm glow of the tiny bulbs against the dark blue of the sky.

She gets to The Touch first, sits down, and waits a few minutes. Then there's a hand on her shoulder and Sammy's there, all six feet and coppery chestnut hair and square jaw of him. There's a hug, a kiss on the cheek, a smile. He's such a guy, she thinks. Just a plain old guy. Being with him is like being in the kitchen of a familiar house, knowing where everything is.

She watches him with real affection while he orders his Buffalo wings. When he looks at the menu and then up at Molly, she flashes back to the way he looked up at her months and months ago, when she was arched over him and her knees were pinning his hips beneath her. While she smiles at him over the table she's thinking about the first time. They started kissing at seven at night and finally did it at four-thirty the next morning. Molly saw the digital clock next to his bed.

She played those hours over in her head for days, shivering with memory. Now she shivers again remembering the time he rolled off her whispering, "Jesus Christ, girl, Jesus Christ," and the time she cried when she came beneath him. She remembers the soft fuzz of his chest against her back, the precision of his movements. And she remembers his mouth, with the softest lips she has ever felt, and her own mouth, too. Now Molly thinks of all the places on Sam's body where her mouth has been, this mouth that is now chatting aimlessly at him.

"What's up?" she says. She wiggles her toes in her shoes even though he can't see them because it makes her feel cute and he likes her cute.

He talks about grad school, his new apartment, his dog. Then he clears his throat and says, "I'm in kind of a relationship right now. I met somebody."

Molly checks his expression. It's awkward, not self-satisfied. He thought she should know. Well, that's okay then.

"That's fine, that's great," she says. "I'm happy for you. I hope it works out."

His face opens up, although he's flustered. Sammy, the guy who does what he ought to do despite how awkward it makes him feel, like some archaic man of real honor. "Thank you," he says. Molly reaches for his hand, grabs it, and says, "It's fine. We had a good time together. It's okay." She's still thinking of his mouth.

"That's a very nice thing to say," he fumbles. It's the most effusive thing he can manage. She's so proud of him for it. For a second she considers asking him, Do you remember? Do you remember the first time? You were never awkward or uptight when we were doing *that*. But she doesn't ask; she knows it would disturb this delicate thread of comfort that is stretched between them.

"Okay, so enough me," he says. "You. What's going on?"

Now what can I say? she thinks. If I'm all alone and no one's watching, she could say, I'll get this idea. It will surface like a bright little silver fish quietly nosing up through the crevices in my brain. I can ignore it and it will pass. But it will come back.

She has learned that. It will always come back, like Jason in *Friday the 13th*. It won't go away completely until something is done about it. A tension grows between doing it and not doing it. There are two marble pillars: slicing and not slicing. And between them is a single strand of dental floss, and it winds tighter and tighter around the pillars, thinner and thinner, stretching until it frays and almost breaks, and finally the strain is unbearable, and Molly has to snip it at one end or the other, to get some kind of relief, so she cuts.

Sam orders microbrewery beer for both of them and as they talk, part of Molly's brain is far away, trying to figure out this attraction she has to cold, silver edges, why she needs to press them against the translucent skin of her wrists. She understands why medieval doctors thought leeches would cure illness; if she were to apply them selectively, in the ancient way, maybe they would suck from her body the poisoned element that courses through her. Maybe they would give her relief, let her rest.

She will die of this, this thing that more and more frequently rises and swells within her until it bursts, this thing that eggs her on to cut, that will not leave her in peace until she has drawn blood. She wonders if this is how cancer patients feel when they realize that this disease and no other will be the one to kill them. There is terror, yes, but also the calm of finally knowing.

What would it be like to be Sammy instead? To worry about telling an old girlfriend about a new girlfriend, instead of about being left alone with a set of knives?

Molly tries her hardest to be lively over her beer. She doesn't want Sam to worry that she's upset about the girlfriend. She wants him to be relaxed and content. But soon she can't help feeling quiet. She tells him she's tired from getting all of her projects in on time. Which is true, she has spent a lot of time at the studio this winter. The order and precision of the architectural models, their elegant structure and the way their joints fit together, seem to calm her. In the last few days, though, she has rushed through her work there, afraid of getting caught with the X-Actos. She says she's also been stressed getting ready for the holidays. She and Liberty are going to have a Christmas dinner with some friends and rent *Monty Python's Life of Brian*.

After a while, she says, "I'm fading," and Sammy says he'll walk partway home with her. They head out.

They stop at the florist and Sam buys her a sunflower. "What the hell," he says as he hands it to her, "I'm a great guy."

"You are so nice, Sammy," Molly says. She kisses his cheek. She admires him for his tact, for knowing the perfect thing to give her. Not red roses or mistletoe. That would be weird. That wouldn't be what he means. He means *warm*, he means *you're still okay with me*, so he gives her a sunflower. Sammy says what he means, simply, and people can understand him.

Sammy, she wants to say to him, why can't I talk?

"What else are you doing tonight?" Sam asks as they walk on.

"*Charlie Brown Christmas* is on at seven."

He nods. "I remember that."

"How about you?"

"Not much. Wrapping presents, stuff like that."

At Molly's corner they hug good-bye and she walks another half block. Then she turns and calls, "Hey, Sammy!" at his retreating back.

"Yeah?"

"Sammy." She smiles up at him as he walks toward her, at his face, his shining hair, his warm mouth.

What language does that mouth speak? she wonders. It speaks the official language, the one in which the usual emotional business is conducted. It speaks the language of normalcy, while

Molly speaks only a pidgin or creole. Not even that, because her language has no other speakers. Some people may understand her, but even among them she knows that each of them is fluent only in his or her own obscure dialect. They share a language common only in its familiarity with shame. And although the language of normalcy is the same everywhere, the language of shame is different for everyone who speaks it.

"Sammy," she says again. What she wants is to stretch out her arms to him. Oh, hey, Sammy, she wants to say. Teach me to talk like you. We hear the same things but people like you know what they mean and I don't. I know it looks like I do but I don't. And I want to so bad. I want to so much that the wanting almost bursts in me and I have to slit my skin open to let it out. Would you take care of me, if you saw the red lines on my arms? Would anyone? We were lovers once, baby, it was so sweet, so fine, and doesn't that count for something? Can't you help me? Sammy, I'm so scared. Talk to me. Help me. And Jesus God, don't leave me alone in the house with all those slick, cruel, beautiful knives.

"*Charlie Brown* is on pretty soon," is what comes out. "You want to come back and watch it with me? It's only half an hour."

He considers, looks at his watch, shrugs, says, "Sure."

She turns on all the lights in the house and puts out Christmas candy and chips and salsa and more beer, and the tail end of the news fills the place with sound. She and Sam get a little more buzzed and flirtatious, and just before the special starts, Liberty comes home, full of stories of horrible people who have tortured the waiters while she cooks, cooks, cooks all day. She breaks out vodka and cranberry juice.

Sam follows Molly into the kitchen when she goes for more candy. "When are you leaving?" she asks. She means, When is your flight, when are you heading home?

"Tomorrow," he sighs. "I tried to get out of it."

"Don't you want to?" It seems so enviably normal. To go home for Christmas. Sam starts to say something, but stops himself.

"Let's just leave that alone," he says. He laughs.

"We didn't know each other last Christmas," Molly answers him, then is flustered because she hadn't meant to say that out loud. It was only a thought that was occurring to her. She didn't know him last Christmas. She's never seen him on a birthday, or met him in the company of his family. She's fucked him every which way from Sunday, but come to think of it, she doesn't know him all that well.

He seems to have decided to say what he was going to say, after all. "Do you ever feel," he says, leaning in close to her, the sweet vodka on his breath, "like everyone else knows some language that you don't know, and talks in it, all the time?"

The Charlie Brown music starts, so she doesn't answer him, she doesn't say, "Oh, baby, I know, I know," but she thinks it, and they both snap to and run into the living room, where Liberty is waiting for them, so they won't miss even a minute. Sam, extra sure of himself on the liquor, plops down between Liberty and Molly in the middle of the couch. They both snuggle up against him. So there he is, beer and vodka and candy canes on the beat-up coffee table in front of him, his arms around two pretty young women. And Molly thinks, Well, where's the harm in that if it gives him some pleasure for an evening? Here we all are, and I'm warm, and I'm safe. So tonight I don't think I'm going to cut myself up. I don't think that will happen, and really, isn't that enough? Can you ask for more? To be safe and warm and cheerful and fairly sure you're not going to hurt yourself for the next eight hours or so, relatively certain you won't need to drag knife blades across your wrists? Isn't that the most that even the healthiest people can have? That's all you can really want.

It's a kind and a generous night, and she doesn't think she'll feel that usual sinking stone in herself when Sammy leaves and the house is suddenly less lively, and she's alone in her room. She and Liberty will probably leave the TV on all night for company and get buzzed and maybe stoned and talk about their families and love, about hard times and art and the role of women. The world is full of warmth.

Now the Peanuts are decorating that poor little tree, because all it needed was a little love, and hollering "Merry Christmas, Charlie Brown!" and singing "Hark! The Herald Angels Sing." They "ooh" their way through it the first time and all stop to take a breath at the exact same moment, every little Peanut cartoon mouth forming a perfect O, just like Molly and Sam and Liberty remember. Then they break, riotously, into the verse. Joyful all ye nations rise, everything's all right, yes everything's fine, Molly thinks, and yes Virginia there is a Santa Claus, and everybody get together try to love one another right now, because all you need is love, and merry Christmas, oh, merry Christmas Charlie Brown, and Lucy and Linus and all of you, and God bless us every one, that's right, she thinks, and fuck you if that's too sentimental for you. God bless us, every one.

❊ ❊ ❊

Very early the next morning, as the light turns pale blue, Molly dreams she is at a special screening of a movie. The leading actress is supposed to answer questions after the show, but she won't; she just stands there on the stage and chatters about nothing. When she finally leaves the theater, Molly chases her outside. A swan flies smoothly overhead with a pale ribbon attached to its foot. Molly catches the ribbon and lowers the swan to her shoulder, and the actress finally turns and listens to her.

"I want to ask you something," says Molly. She sees the actress's crow's feet from the sun, the small imperfections in her beauty.

"I want to know," she picks up again, "will this always be? Will I always be sick? Do I need a shot of something every morning, like insulin? Do I need a needle in my arm? Can I do anything except prolong my life? Or will I be well?"

The actress answers telepathically, without words.

Molly awakes. She is inhaling and exhaling very fast and her open mouth is dry. She is disturbed, but she is not frightened. She has lost track of the swan.

She can't remember the actress's answer to her question. She sits up and examines the tender flesh on the insides of her elbows. How deep, she wonders, is a cut when it needs a stitch? She lies back down, putting her head in the crook of her arm and feeling there the silkiness of her hair.

There are so many things in her life that she wishes hadn't happened, weren't real, weren't part of her memory or anybody else's. Painful things, humiliating things, hard things, the same as everybody has. But she knows there's nothing you can do to make it so that those things didn't happen. Which is the only thing that will help. Sometimes it's not enough to heal something, you just want the thing not to be. That's the reason people kill themselves, Molly thinks. To make things that are real no longer real, if only in their own minds, which will never again remember. To go back to long, long ago. Suicide, she realizes now, is just a clumsy attempt at time travel.

Peace on earth and mercy mild.

There is a dictionary across the room, in a stack with all the textbooks and drafting supplies. Molly gets out of bed and sits cross-legged on the floor. She opens the dictionary, so distinguished and courtly with its gilt edges and golden title, and scans the columns, shuffling through the pages, searching, searching, searching, to look up the word "mercy."

ACKNOWLEDGMENTS

First, I would like to say thank you to a special group of my past and present colleagues and friends, the ladies of Jossey-Bass's Editorial Production Department, who were there for the genesis of so many of these stories: Susan Abel, Elizabeth Forsaith, Marcella Friel, Michele Hubinger, Xenia Lisanevich, Gigi Mark, Alice Rowan, Laurel Scheinman, Lasell Whipple, and Lorri Wimer. The Falling Nun salutes you all!

I have many other friends and well-wishers whom I cannot thank enough for their support as I began—and continue on—the road to writing: Neil Bason, Tom Bemis, Cathy Bowman, Michael Crowley, Susan Eigenbrodt, Dorothy Hearst, Judith Hibbard, Leslie Katz, Pam MacLean, Tom Murphy, Erika Nanes, Carolyn Uno, Lisa Vega, and Jeff Wyneken. It is not hyperbole when I say that I could not have written this book, or any other, without them. Add to this my dear friend who has been my teacher in writing and all matters of life, Philip Herter; my talented role model, a remarkable woman in every way, Robin Maxwell; and my lovely, warm, and wonderful sister, Brenna Hopkins. There is one more group of friends I wish to thank, who helped me with these stories more than they know: David Karppinen, Daria Labinsky, Nancy Ozeri, Jefre Parker, and Adrienne Pataki.

Thank you to my father and mother, who, as I grew up, never

had to have it explained to them *why* someone would want to be a writer—or a poet or a painter or an actor or a dancer. I did not know then how rare that is.

Peter Turchi at the Warren Wilson MFA Program for Writers deserves special thanks from me for running that remarkable place and for his personal encouragement (I'm not forgetting the two extra weeks he once gave me to pay my tuition!). And how can I properly thank my advisers there? Robert Boswell, Joan Silber, Chuck Wachtel, and especially C. J. Hribal were so generous and taught me so much. Thank you from the bottom of my heart, also, to all the talented writers at Warren Wilson and elsewhere who took the time to teach me or to give me an encouraging word: Andrea Barrett, Charles Baxter, Karen Brennan, Thaisa Frank, Kevin McIlvoy, Rick Russo, Lisa Shea, Susan Vreeland, and Geoffrey Wolff.

Thank you to my stellar editors, Kris Puopolo and Nicole Diamond, who always pushed me to make my work the best it could be. I owe them much. I also want to take an opportunity to thank my fabulous, my fantastic, my superlative agent, Jenny Bent, who is everything I dreamed an agent would be and more, a wonderful person and friend. And my compliments to my terrific copyeditor, George Wen, and production editor, Jay Schweitzer, as well as publicist extraordinaire Kimberly Saunders.

Finally, last but very definitely not least, I want to say thank you to my husband, the most talented, kind, handsome, intelligent, and wonderful man I know. My books would not be there without his support and love.

THE FALLING NUN

1. In "Tat," Liberty has a religious experience of sorts during her time in the tattoo parlor, and gets a glimpse of a universe where "it seems to her that everyone she knows is so full of love and suffering, so very full, that it overflows into wounds." What is it about getting her tattoo that leaves Liberty feeling so at peace? How does Jack, in his role as a guide, help Liberty experience this feeling?

2. "She moved toward him, and away from him, and toward him, and away from him, and in going toward him she was also going away from him, and maybe he was doing the same." This description of the dynamic between Elizabeth and Vinnie in "Gold Glitter," while specifically sexual in this instance, could easily describe the dynamic between other characters in this collection as well, as they constantly test the boundaries and either shy away from or take risks with their interpersonal relationships. In what ways is this quote representative of larger issues? Keeping this hot/cold, push/pull dynamic in mind, do you think honesty or commitment is possible for the people in these stories?

3. In a sense, it seems that Ronnie in "Veronica" is actively trying *not* to believe, chanting what almost seems like a prayer in and of itself: "I don't believe, I don't believe." Do you think Ronnie is a believer? Is there any resolution to the girl's struggle by the end of the story? Do you think Sister Veronica's confession will add to Ronnie's confusion, to her further disillusionment with her faith, or will it somehow help to relieve it?

4. "There is such a thing as sisterhood, isn't there?" questions the narrator in "The Falling Nun." How are relationships between women presented in this book? What do the women in these stories need from each other that they can't get from men? Anything? Does sisterhood, in fact, exist at all? Which friendships between women seem fulfilling and healthy, and which are somehow lacking? What are the complexities in each type of relationship?

5. As Ramon kisses Miranda in "Bethlehem" she "feels something intangible, like light, a glow, a soft diffusion, traveling from Ramon's mouth to hers." In what ways does this quote shed light on Ramon's function in the story? Is he reminiscent of other characters in this collection? Has Miranda found salvation in the end?

What is it about Ramon that allows him to succeed in the face of obvious clinical depression when doctors and prescriptions have failed?

6. "Witch" pulls the reader into the fantastical vision of the narrator, a vision that straddles the "make believe" world of witches and potions, and the "real life" world of ballet, school, and parents. To what extent did you question the narrator's view of the world around her? Keeping in mind that her twin grows up to be a "normal" woman, who is ultimately disapproving and frightened of her sister, discuss whether this is a modern-day fairy tale, or if it is a journey into the mind of a madwoman. Are the two mutually exclusive?

7. In the story "Snakes" the narrator speaks of a "metal box, deeply, deeply buried beneath the flesh . . . and I could take nothing else inside myself but what went in this box." What do you make of the box imagery? What are the "other things" in the box that she vaguely refers to knowing about? How does this tie into her mother and her paralyzing fear of snakes?

8. Early on in "Men Have More Upper Body Strength," what elements set the tone for the rest of the story and highlight the gender dynamics that are at work here? Did you find it surprising and/or refreshing to see women, who are often portrayed as victims, acting as predators?

9. Brigid's motivations in this story have nothing to do with sex or desire: "She felt nothing that reminded her of arousal. She wasn't going to come and she knew it. She wasn't even turned on. She didn't care. That had nothing to do with anything." Why do you think Brigid unleashes the total force of her resentment and rage onto Boniface, not only raping him but wanting to punch him in the mouth and humiliate him?

10. In "Holy Holy Holy" it seems that serious faith is somehow humorous or "a good party story," which is how the narrator describes her Catholic school days and the prayer that the temp offered for her carpal tunnel syndrome. What is it about religion that strikes the narrator and the other party guests as absurd or funny? How does the quote from *The Revelation of St. John the Divine*, which is one of only two quotes to start off a story, shed light on the ending? Why does the narrator break down crying?

11. What is the significance of "Playing Crucifixion" for the boy in this story? How does this strange game tie into his feelings for his father and his longing to know John Robert Flynn, a man who, like Jesus, made "the Supreme Sacrifice"?

12. Discuss the parallels between "Tat" and "Merry Christmas, Charlie Brown," the first and last stories in this collection, looking not

only at obvious character overlap but at the larger ideological and spiritual themes that they share. What exactly are these two women searching for in seemingly different ways—Liberty through piercing and tattoos, and Molly through cutting? Does the idea of flagellation and achievement through suffering materialize in other stories as well?

Pamela Rafael Berkman's
debut collection of stories
celebrates the women
in Shakespeare's world.

0-7432-1255-X/ $12.00